**'Well, thanks for your advice, Gabe. I think you've covered everything.'**

But now he seemed reluctant to drop the subject. His deep voice penetrated the night. 'Piper, you're not afraid of intimacy, are you?'

Without warning her blood began to pound through her veins, making her ears hum and her heart beat wildly. 'I—I don't think so.' But she couldn't be sure. Her limited experience of kissing had ranged from mildly pleasant to downright mortifying. Staring at her hands, still clenched tightly in her lap, she added softly, 'I don't know. I might be.'

She sensed him moving towards her and the next moment his fingertips were touching her cheek, ever so gently. She was amazed how good it felt. Beneath his touch her skin felt different, highly sensitised, alive in a whole new way. His thumb reached her mouth and began to trace the outline of her lower lip. Then stopped. No! She didn't want it to stop. Hardly believing her daring, she dipped her head slightly and pressed her lips to his thumb.

Gabe's husky voice sounded close to her ear. 'I think you know a lot more about touching than you're letting on...'

**Barbara Hannay** was born in Sydney, educated in Brisbane and has spent most of her adult life living in tropical North Queensland, where she and her husband have raised four children. While she has enjoyed many happy times camping and canoeing in the bush, she also delights in an urban lifestyle—chamber music, contemporary dance, movies and dining out. An English teacher, she has always loved writing, and now, by having her stories published, she is living her most cherished fantasy.

**Recent titles by the same author:**

A BRIDE AT BIRRALEE
THEIR DOORSTEP BABY
THE WEDDING DARE
THE PREGNANCY DISCOVERY

# A WEDDING AT WINDAROO

BY

BARBARA HANNAY

*First published in Great Britain 2003*
*Harlequin Mills & Boon Limited,*
*Eton House, 18-24 Paradise Road, Richmond, Surrey TW9 1SR*



ISBN 0 263 17654 1

*Set in Times Roman 10½ on 12 pt.*
*07-0203-45950*

*Printed and bound in Great Britain*
*by Antony Rowe Ltd, Chippenham, Wiltshire*

# PROLOGUE

THREE weeks past her twelfth birthday, Piper O'Malley spent almost an entire afternoon huddled behind the tractor shed crying. And the stupid thing was she hated crying! Crying was for girls and today she didn't want to be a girl.

By the time Gabe Rivers found her she'd reduced her sobs to the occasional sniffle, but she knew her eyes were still red and swollen.

'Hey, cheer up, tree frog,' he said, crouching beside her and throwing a strong, comforting arm around her skinny shoulders. 'Nothing's ever as bad as it seems.'

She swiped her eyes with her shirt-tail. 'It is today. This is the worst day of my life.'

He looked so surprised she made a hasty amendment. After all, Gabe was eighteen—and like all adults he had a way of knowing when you weren't telling the exact truth. 'I suppose the very worst day of my life must have been when Mum and Dad died, but I was too little to remember.'

'But this is the second worst day?' he asked. 'Sounds bad. What's the problem?'

She burrowed her face against his big shoulder. 'I can't tell you. It's too awful.'

'Course you can. I'm unshockable.'

Peeping up at him she found his green eyes regarding her so tenderly she felt her heart swell. 'Periods,' she whispered.

'I see,' he said after a beat. 'Well...yeah...that's tough, I guess.'

She half expected Gabe to leap away from her, to tell her that now he'd finished helping her grandfather with branding and ear-tagging calves he needed to hurry home to Edenvale. But he stayed right beside her. They sat for ages with their backs against the corrugated iron wall of the tractor shed, chewing fresh, sweet stalks of grass and watching the daylight soften as the afternoon slipped away.

'You'll get used to the idea after a while,' he told her.

'I won't, Gabe. I know I won't ever. Why do I have to be a girl? I wish I was a boy. I want to be like you.'

He grinned. 'And what's so good about being like me?'

'Everything,' she cried with the wholehearted sincerity of a true hero-worshipper. 'You're bigger and stronger than Grandad, and he never tries to stop you from doing *anything*. And you can be whatever you want to be. When I grow up I'm going to have to have babies and wash some man's smelly old socks and underpants.'

Gabe laughed. 'Wait till you go to boarding school next term. Your teachers will tell you that girls have the same chance to be anything they want to these days.'

'But I want to be a cattleman. Bet you never heard anyone talk about a cattle*woman*, have you?'

He chuckled playfully and pulled her akubra down over her eyes. When she knocked the broad-brimmed hat back into place she was surprised to see the laughter in his eyes die. Suddenly he was looking sad and serious.

'What's the matter?'

He shook his head. 'Nothing you need worry about, mouse.'

'Come on, Gabe. I told you my horrible secret and I

haven't even told Miriam, my best girlfriend. If you tell me, I won't tell anyone else.'

He smiled at her—as if he was seeing right inside her and really liked what he found. 'Well,' he said slowly, 'guys can have their own problems, you know.'

'Like having to shave?'

He grinned. 'That's one of them. But it gets worse.'

'Going bald?'

'I'm not talking about that kind of stuff. I mean it's not always that easy for us blokes to do just whatever we want. My dad expects me to stay on Edenvale for ever.'

'Of course.' She frowned at him. 'What's wrong with that?'

He grimaced. 'This will probably shock you, but I don't want to be a cattleman.'

'You're kidding.' She was shocked. Shocked to the soles of her riding boots. Her belly, which was already feeling sore, bunched into a nervous knot. How could anyone reject the wonderful life of a cattleman? If Gabe didn't want to run cattle, what on earth could he want? And where did he want to go? The possibility that he might not stay right next door on Edenvale for ever scared her.

'What do you want to do?'

'That!' he said, pointing to a giant wedgetail eagle circling high above them. Piper watched it with him and admired the strength of its dark V-shaped wings as it climbed higher and higher into the fading blue of the afternoon sky. Eventually, the slow, steady wings stopped moving altogether as the bird worked the thermals, gliding free. Then it was still in the air, hovering in one place.

Gabe's face was alight with excitement. 'Isn't that

fantastic? I'd give anything to learn to fly like that, to soar or hover with that much freedom. That much power and control. I'm sick of being tied to the ground with a mob of dusty, dumb cattle.'

It was a side to Gabe that she'd never seen before, never guessed. 'Where could you learn to fly?'

'An army recruitment fellow was in Mullinjim last week.' His glowing face was still fixed on the eagle, watching it grow smaller and smaller as it climbed away again. 'They'll sign me up and train me to fly helicopters—Black Hawks.'

He stared after the bird with such an intense longing that even at her tender age Piper could see the finality of his choice. She knew instinctively that although it was the kind of dream that would take him away, probably for ever, it was the kind of dream Gabe had to follow.

The knot of fear in the pit of her stomach tightened. She wished she was older and less afraid, and hoped he couldn't see that she was falling apart at the thought of his going away.

'So what's the problem?' she asked in a shaky, not-quite-brave voice. 'Won't your family let you leave?'

His face twisted into a grimace of pain. 'They're not at all happy about the idea, but I'm going, Piper. I'm quite settled in my mind about that.'

She did her very best to smile.

# CHAPTER ONE

*Eleven years later…*

IT SHOULD have been a perfect night.

Piper loved to be out in the bush after dark, when the hard sun retreated, the clean, sharp scent of eucalyptus lingered on the cooling air and the slender gum trees stretched silver-white limbs up to the moon.

And tonight Gabe was back.

So everything *would* have been perfect if she hadn't been stressed to the eyeballs. But tension had been building inside her all evening and now the strain was unbearable.

She'd been practising in her head what she needed to ask Gabe, and no matter which words she chose they all sounded pathetic. But she had to get them out, had to speak now before she chickened out again.

Closing her eyes, she took a deep breath, then released it in a rush. 'Gabe, I need your help. I need to find a husband.'

Oh, blast! Her request sounded even more ridiculous out loud than it had when she'd been practising. But it was too late to take the words back. All she could do now was wait for his response.

Wait…

And wait some more…while she crouched beside

him in the dark and watched the surrounding paddocks for the first signs of cattle thieves.

If only she could see his face! But the moonlight couldn't reach their hiding place behind a huge granite boulder.

'Gabe?' she whispered.

Maybe he thought her question was just too silly to warrant an answer. She should drop the whole crazy subject now. After all, he had only come home a few days ago and already she'd asked him to help her catch cattle duffers. She could hardly blame the man if he balked at solving her personal dilemmas as well.

His riding boots crunched small stones as he shifted his weight slightly, and then his voice came rumbling through the dark. 'Since when have you had an urge to find a husband?'

She winced when she heard the mocking edge to his tone. If only she could check out his hard, handsome face. Was he laughing at her?

'Just—recently.' As recently as last night—after her grandfather had told her his shocking news.

Again Gabe didn't answer. Instead he stood up and stretched cramped limbs. He walked a few paces away, moving into the bright light cast by the full moon, and she saw his grimace as he flexed his right knee.

Anyone who didn't know about his accident would see a ruggedly athletic man—tall, lean-hipped and strong shouldered, with short, military-style black hair and a hard jaw shadowed by overnight stubble.

The stiffness in his right leg was the only sign that his tough and rugged exterior had taken a battering. It was easy to forget that he was recovering from a car crash that had forced him out of the army and almost taken his life.

Snagging a stalk of pale Mitchell grass, he rolled it between his fingers, stepped closer again and tickled her nose with it. 'What's this about looking for a husband? You're not old enough to get married.'

'Rubbish. I'm twenty-three.'

He looked startled. 'Are you really?'

'Sure am.'

Seconds ticked by while he frowned at a nearby brigalow bush, as if he needed to digest this news. She wondered why he seemed so surprised. He'd been six years old when she was born. And he was quite good at arithmetic.

'Why the rush?' he asked at last.

'Marriage is my only solution, Gabe.'

'Solution to what?' He sounded understandably puzzled.

'Last night—Grandad told me—' Her voice broke as the tears she'd been battling over the past twenty-four hours rushed to fill her eyes and throat. She'd been trying to hold back this news, but it was only fair that she explain. 'The doctors have told him that another heart attack will almost certainly be one—one too many.'

The immense sadness she'd been shouldering all day sent her lurching towards him. And good old Gabe tossed the grass stalk aside and held out his arms to her.

It seemed perfectly natural to hurl herself into the open arms of her oldest friend—absolutely right for him to draw her head onto his big, bulky shoulder. He was wearing an old woollen jumper that made him feel soft and huge and comforting, just what she needed right now.

'Are they saying they've done all they can?' he asked gently.

She nodded against his shoulder. 'He's had three operations in the last five years, and test after test...'

Gabe sighed. 'I'm surprised they put it to him so bluntly.'

'You know what Grandad's like. He would have forced them to give him the truth with no frills attached.'

'And I guess he wants to prepare you now. You know how much he loves you.'

'I know,' she sobbed. 'And he doesn't want me to worry about him or make a fuss.' Her nose emitted a loud, unladylike snort as she fought off another onslaught of tears. She lifted her head. 'But the other bad news is that he doesn't think I can manage Windaroo on my own. He's planning to sell this place.'

Again Gabe took ages to speak. 'I guess Michael would worry if he left you trying to carry on here by yourself.'

'But I can't believe he wants to sell this property! It's bad enough knowing that I'm going to lose him, but I can't bear the thought of losing Windaroo as well.' She drew a shuddering breath. 'I've worked so hard to keep this place going and I love it.'

And that was the understatement of the century. She'd always felt that she shared Windaroo's life blood.

Through tear-blurred eyes she looked over Gabe's shoulder to the fat white moon and the wide, star-stippled outback sky. She was trusting her old friend to understand how devastated she felt, but maybe she was asking too much of him. After all, he'd been away in the army for ten long years, and he'd had his own problems during twelve months in and out of hospital.

He loosened his hold on her and leaned back so that he could read her face. 'So you think that if you find a bloke to marry you Michael will change his mind about selling Windaroo?'

She sighed and stepped away from him. If she wanted Gabe's help she needed to explain this very clearly. 'It's the only solution I can think of. Men of Grandad's generation can't come to terms with the idea of leaving a girl in charge of a cattle station. A husband would make all the difference.'

'I guess you're right.' He looked at her sharply again. 'I suppose marriage could be a solution. But it's a mighty big step.'

'I know. That's why I could do with some help.'

'But Piper, for Pete's sake—' Gabe shook his head. 'Why the blue blazes would you need *my* help to catch a man?'

She gulped and looked away. Time to swallow her pride and make a painful confession. ''Cause the guys around here don't seem to have noticed I'm female.'

He had the bad grace to chuckle. Loudly—and for far longer than was necessary.

Piper slapped his arm. 'I'm serious. Your brother Jonno and the rest of them—they just don't think of me as a woman.'

'Oh, Piper,' Gabe wheezed between chuckles. 'You *can't* be serious.'

'Why would I make up something like that? Honestly, the fellows around here just see me as one of them, and I'm sick of it.'

'But no one could think you were a bloke. You're so—so—little. Besides, we all *know* you're a girl.' Thumbs loosely hooked in the belt loops at his hips, he stared at her. 'You're not joking, are you?'

She almost stamped her foot. 'Of course not!'

'Well, I think you're wrong.'

'How would you know, Gabe? When was the last time you came to a party out this way? You wouldn't have a clue. The problem is that because I can muster with the men, and I can leg-rope a bullock or turn a baby bull into a steer, they forget I'm a girl. They don't even *try* to crack on to me. I have buddy status and that's all. I'm just good mates with them—the way I am with you.'

Gabe's smirk faded and he rubbed his chin thoughtfully. 'Well...you have to remember that blokes like to be able to impress a woman. Maybe your problem is that you can do everything they can—and you do it too damn well.'

'I hope you're not suggesting I become weak and useless.'

His gaze ran over her and he grinned. 'Heaven forbid.' Then he turned and cast a long, searching look over his shoulder at the surrounding paddocks before glancing at his watch.

Piper sighed. They'd been out here for four hours and there'd been no hint of cattle duffers. Gabe was probably thinking that her request for help to stake them out had simply been a ruse to get him on his own so she could regale him with her problems about the opposite sex.

'I can't promise the duffers will show up tonight,' she said. 'But they usually strike at full moon, when it's easier for them to work.'

On the last full moon Windaroo cattle had been taken from a holding yard near a bore on the southern boundary, and a similar thing had happened to a block in the east the previous month.

The duffers had been following a familiar pattern—moving into a remote area and doing a quick muster, then trucking the beasts out of the valley along back roads.

Tonight Piper and Gabe were watching a paddock on the western boundary. She'd seen the tracks of trail bikes there a few days ago, and suspected that someone was casing the area.

'At least we can make ourselves more comfortable,' she said, thinking of his bad leg, which was probably much more painful than he let on. 'We can spread our swags out here and I can bribe you with soup.'

Together they found flat ground, flicked stones away and unrolled their canvas swags and bedding. Piper rummaged in her backpack, extracted a Thermos and filled two mugs with hot, fragrant, homemade tomato soup.

'Sorry to dump my hassles on you,' she said, after she'd taken her first warming sip.

'No need to apologise.' Gabe grinned. 'I'm used to it.'

And wasn't that the truth? Just sitting here with Gabe, having him home again, made her remember all the times she'd come to him with her problems. And how desperately lonely she'd felt when he left. She'd never really understood Gabe's urge to get away, but she knew that somehow it had reinforced in her an even stronger desire to stay on Windaroo—as if she'd needed to prove to him and to herself that life out here was worthwhile, worth fighting for.

'That's a long face,' he said, pulling her sharply back from her thoughts.

She smiled and shrugged. 'I've got a lot to think about.'

He set his soup mug on the ground and his gaze held hers. He wasn't in shadow any more, and in the moonlight his eyes were dark and brooding rather than the lively green she knew them to be. 'You don't need to worry about finding a husband, Piper.'

She groaned. 'Don't tell me you think I should give in and let Grandad sell Windaroo?'

'Under certain circumstances it could be a good idea.'

'What kind of circumstances?'

'What if…what if I were to buy Windaroo? Michael would sell it to me.'

Surprise sent such a savage jolt through her that she almost dropped her mug. She had a blinding, instantaneous vision of herself and Gabe living for ever on Windaroo, running the property—working partners and steadfast friends way into their old age. Now *that* was a dream she could live with! 'Would you really want to do that?' she asked in a hushed, awe-filled whisper.

'Well, it's a possibility. I know Jonno's interested in buying out my shares in the Edenvale property, and I've a substantial payout from the army. I'm looking for an investment. I could buy Windaroo and hire some extra hands, appoint you as manager, and you could go on living here and running the place for as long as you want to.'

She frowned. 'But what about you? What would you do?'

He shrugged and she saw a shadowy bitterness tighten his features. 'I'm not sure. I haven't decided what I want to do with the rest of my life yet. I can't fly Black Hawks any more, but I could train helicopter pilots for cattle mustering, or I could set up my own chopper mustering business. Or there's always the city. I still have quite a few options up my sleeve.'

Cradling her cooling mug in both hands, she drew circles in the dust with the heel of her riding boot and tried to shake off a crazy sense of disappointment. Of course Gabe didn't want to settle down and live here. He'd left the bush because he craved adventure.

Why would he want to live on this rundown property with her when there was an enticing world beyond the Mullinjim Valley? A world of excitement, adventure and sophisticated, sexy women.

How could she have let herself forget that Gabriel Rivers was a cool, tough Black Hawk hero and a knock-em-dead lady-killer?

She swallowed the lump of pain in her throat. 'Your offer is very generous, Gabe, but I don't really like the idea. I—I don't want to be a tenant on my family's land. It would feel all wrong. Can you see that?'

'But I thought you wanted to stay here no matter what.'

'I do, but it would be best if I could find a husband. Then Grandad wouldn't need to sell the property and it would still be mine. Well…mine and the husband's, I guess, but at least it would still be in the family.'

He stared at something way off in the distance. 'It was just a thought.'

'That's why I was hoping you could give me some sure-fire hints about how to catch a guy.'

Slowly his gaze swung back to her, and now he stared at her for ages. For far too long. 'I'm the wrong man for that job, Piper.'

She let out a disbelieving little laugh. 'Oh, come on, Gabe. You're an expert. I'm expecting a master class from you. Everyone out here knows what a hit you made with the women in the big smoke. We got sick of hearing about your big city reputation as a babe magnet.'

'A babe magnet?' With a toss of his head he released a wry sound that she guessed was a laugh.

'The stories were flying thick and fast about how those city girls took one look at your country boy swagger and were panting all over you.'

'You shouldn't listen to gossip.'

'I didn't need to. I saw with my own eyes what happened every time you came home on leave. Remember the ''babe pack''? That gang of city girls who followed you out here just to take a look at you doing your cowboy act?'

With a sigh of irritation at the distasteful memory, she picked up the empty mugs and stacked them next to her backpack.

As Gabe watched he asked, 'You haven't seen any girls following me this time, have you?'

'No,' she admitted softly, and she bit her lip, wondering if she'd touched a sore point. Whenever she and her grandfather had travelled to the city to visit Gabe in hospital she'd never seen any of the trendy city girlfriends. As far as she could tell, not one of Gabe's 'babe pack' had shown the staying power necessary to see him through the long, painful months of recovery and rehabilitation after the accident.

'You know,' she said, searching for a change of subject, 'Grandad reckons it's his fault I've turned into a tomboy. He says he never got around to putting the right finishing touches on me.'

'What kind of finishing touches does he want?'

'He thinks he should have sent me off to the city when I left school instead to letting me come straight back here to start work as a jillaroo. Says I should have gone to university, or overseas on one of those exchanges—some place where I could mix with other young people. He thinks I should have broadened my horizons—the way you have.'

Gabe nodded. 'Maybe it's not too late. You could do it now. If you're determined to find a husband there are millions of blokes to choose from in cities all along the coast.'

She sighed. 'But what use would a city guy be to me? I need a cattleman for a husband not a geeky banker or a computer nerd.' She kicked at a stone and sent it scudding into the dark. 'Choice isn't my problem. There's no shortage of eligible blokes in the bush. My problem is that I don't know how to *start* husband-hunting. I've never been into proper girly stuff. Even at boarding school fashion and make-up never interested me. And I've never worked out how to—to—'

'Flirt?' Gabe inserted with a slow smile.

'Yes.' Her eyes widened as comprehension dawned. 'You're so right. Flirting! That's exactly what I can't do. Gosh, I don't have a clue how to start. But that's what a girl has to do, isn't it—if she wants to let a guy know she's interested?'

Just then a cloud drifted across the moon and they were plunged into darkness. Piper wished she could see Gabe's face. Was he annoyed with her for bringing up such a personal subject? His voice sounded strangely rough and gravelly when he answered. 'I don't think I'm the right person to give you advice. You might learn all the wrong things.'

Wrong things? What wrong things? She thought of the babe pack again, and her cheeks flamed so hotly that she was suddenly grateful for the dark.

But next moment silvery moonlight filtered down, and she could see Gabe eyeing her thoughtfully as he leaned back with his weight supported by his hands while his long legs stretched out in front of him. 'So you want to know how to flirt and how to please a man?' he asked.

She gulped. She hadn't expected that hearing him

speak about this would make her feel quite so shivery and nervous.

Perhaps she should tell him to forget she'd ever raised the subject. She didn't need his advice. Inexperienced as she was, she'd read enough books, seen enough television and listened to enough campfire boasting from ringers to know the anatomical details of sex.

In theory.

But then she remembered the last party she'd been to, when Gabe's brother Jonno had sidled up to her and asked her to put in a good word about him to Suzanne Heath. It had hit her then that the guys were always doing things like that. They saw her simply as a buddy—a good sport—a fast ticket to an introduction to a girl—but never as the object of their desire.

Her eyes met Gabe's.

'I'm sure you don't need flirting lessons,' he said softly. He nodded towards the cattle to their left. 'We'd be better off refining our strategies for dealing with these duffers when they turn up.'

'No,' she responded, a little too quickly. 'I'm sure the duffers are cowards and will be easy to frighten. But what you were saying just now—about how to flirt—and how to—to please a man. That's exactly what I need to know.'

He scowled. 'I wasn't serious.'

'But I am.'

Releasing his breath in a slow hiss, he shook his head. His laugh, when it came, was soft and almost sad. 'Are you calling my bluff, Piper O'Malley?'

'I sure am.'

Oh, man. It was easy enough to sound as if she meant that, but her heart had begun to pound strangely.

## CHAPTER TWO

GABE cleared his throat. 'How to catch a man? Well...let's see.'

A tawny owl winged its way overhead and he stared after it as it disappeared into the night. 'To be honest, I've never really analysed what goes on when a man gets interested in a woman. It seems instinctive.' He scratched the side of his neck thoughtfully. 'But I guess something's actually happening to our senses. They start reacting long before our brain realises what's going on.'

'Your senses? You mean sight, sound—that sort of thing?' She was impressed. This sounded like useful, practical information.

'I think so. I'd say sight would have to be number one for most blokes.'

'Well, there you go. Men don't even notice I'm female, so I don't stand a chance.'

His eyes crinkled at the edges as his gaze slid over her. 'It's a bit hard for guys to see what's available if a girl is always hiding under a wide-brimmed hat, jeans, baggy shirts and high-sided riding boots.'

She wriggled uncomfortably. 'You mean I should be wearing clothes like Suzanne Heath? Dresses that are at least two sizes too small?'

'Who's Suzanne Heath?'

'The chick Jonno was latching onto at a party last month.'

He stiffened like an animal on full alert. 'So you've got your sights set on my little brother?'

'No, not particularly.' She shrugged. 'He's just an example. Just about any guy will do. Remember, I'm desperate.'

Lunging forward quickly, he surprised her by grasping her shoulders. 'Piper,' he said almost savagely, his eyes burning into hers, 'promise me one thing.'

'Yes?' she whispered, forcing the single word past the sudden scary tightness in her throat. What was the matter with Gabe? He looked so fierce.

His hands gripped her hard. 'You're *not* desperate. Don't sell yourself short. You mustn't marry a man you don't love.'

Startled by the ferocity in his eyes and his voice, she dropped her gaze and stared at her hands clenched in her lap as she said, 'Maybe I'll be easy to please.'

'Don't be. Just remember you deserve a good man. A man who'll cherish you.'

Her head shot up. 'Cherish me?'

'Yep. That's what you deserve.' He smiled a shaky, crooked smile and released her shoulders quickly, as if he was surprised to find he'd been gripping her so hard.

'I'll remember that when the time comes,' she said, trying not to sound as shaken as she felt. 'But first I have to get at least one fellow to notice me. The problem is I don't like the clothes men seem to like on women. I hate tight dresses with short skirts and low necklines.'

'Why?'

She felt caught out by his question. 'I—I don't know. They look so uncomfortable.'

'Have you ever worn one?'

'No.'

Gabe's smile looked more secure now. 'It wouldn't hurt to give it a go some time.'

'But girls who wear them have plenty of curves.'

He grinned. 'You go in and out in all the right places.'

She was surprised he'd noticed. But then maybe he was just saying that to make her feel better. 'My ins and outs are very tiny. Do you think it would help if I stuffed my—my chest?'

'Your husband-to-be might not be too happy when he discovers socks shoved down your bra.'

Her mouth tightened into a self-righteous pout. 'By the time he finds out it won't matter. It'll be too late, won't it?'

Gabe shook his head slowly. 'My dear girl, you've got a lot to learn.'

She looked away. There was every chance she'd never find a man she wanted to share such intimate secrets with.

He reached over and flicked her ponytail. 'Take that elastic thing out of your hair.'

'Now?'

'Yeah.'

Uncertainly, she hooked her finger under the elasticised band and slid it down, then shook her shoulder length hair free. Yellow hair, Grandad called it. Her driver's licence said it was fair. A teacher at school had called it strawberry blonde. The biggest problem was that it came with very fair skin that she had to keep covered and out of the sun.

'You should do that more often, Piper. You have very pretty hair. If you let a fellow see all that, especially in the moonlight, you'll...make a big impression.'

'I suppose...'

'No supposing. I mean it—absolutely.'

'So you reckon I need to let my hair down and buy a skimpy dress?'

'It certainly can't hurt to fem things up a bit.'

'OK, assuming I get the looks sorted out, what comes next? What are the other senses? Sound? I don't know if I could manage a low and husky voice for very long.'

He grinned. 'Tell a guy what a great bloke he is and it won't matter much how you sound. Flattery and flirtation go hand in hand. Anyway, you've never been one to screech or cackle. You sound fine.'

'That's a relief. So that brings us to smell. What impresses a guy when it comes to smell?'

'Clean hair, clean skin.'

'Perfume?'

'If it's delicate. Something that enhances your femininity but doesn't get in the way of it.'

'My femininity?' What did *that* smell like?

An unsettling vision floated before her. She saw Gabe with a woman in his arms. A very beautiful woman with long silky hair and superior curves. Someone who smelled feminine. She could picture his sensuous lips caressing her exposed creamy throat, drinking in the smell of her.

An unexpected sound sent the image scattering. A kind of groan. *Shoot!* Had she made that noise? What was wrong with her?

What was wrong with Gabe? He was looking as embarrassed as she felt. Time to move this conversation along. 'I'll remember to make sure my perfume is delicate.' So what senses were left? Sight, sound and smell were covered, so that left touch. Heck, no! She'd have to skip that one. But that only left taste, and no way did she want to know how she was supposed to taste!

'Touch and taste aren't really part of flirting. They don't count, do they?'

'If you're looking for a husband they count for a great deal.'

Something about the way Gabe said that made her feel tight in the chest. 'Well, yes. I suppose they matter when you get past flirting and around to kissing.' She was definitely having trouble breathing. 'Well, thanks for your advice, Gabe. I think you've covered everything.'

But now, darn it, he seemed reluctant to drop the subject. His deep voice penetrated the night. 'Piper, you're not frightened of intimacy, are you?'

Without warning, her blood began to pound through her veins, making her ears hum and her heart thump wildly. 'I—I don't think so.'

But she couldn't be sure. Her limited experiences of kissing and necking ranged from mildly pleasant to downright mortifying. She should remember that this was Gabe, and if there was anyone in the world she could talk to about such embarrassing stuff it was him. Staring at her hands, still clenched tightly in her lap, she added softly, 'I don't know. I might be.'

She sensed him leaning towards her, and next moment his fingertips were touching her cheek ever so gently—so very gently—she could hardly feel them—and she found herself wanting to feel them, needing to feel them, found she was leaning her cheek into the curve of his hand. His big warm hand.

She knew exactly what it looked like. She could picture the strong, square shape of his palm, the light brown hairs on the back of his hand, the long, strong fingers. Eyes closed, she rubbed her cheek against his cupped hand.

She heard the rasp of his breathing and felt his thumb travel slowly down her cheek, over her chin and back again. She was amazed by how good it felt. Exciting, but sweet.

His fingertips circled slowly, ever so slowly over her

cheek, her chin, her lips. Beneath his touch her skin felt different, highly sensitised, alive in a whole new way.

When his thumb moved again it reached her mouth and began to trace the outline of her lower lip. It strolled back and forth, back and forth. Then stopped.

No! She didn't want it to stop. Hardly believing her daring, she dipped her head slightly and pressed her lips to his thumb.

Gabe's husky voice sounded close to her ear. 'I think you know a lot more about touching than you're letting on, moonbeam.'

'No,' she whispered. 'But I want to learn, Gabe.' She pressed parted lips to his thumb again. The tip of her tongue touched his skin and she felt her skin flushing all over with a wild kind of excitement.

She was sure she was burning. Her face was hot. All over her body her skin felt aquiver with heat. Gabe's face was so close, and she wanted to feel the midnight roughness of his beard against her cheek.

She suddenly knew that she needed his lips to roam her face the way his fingers had. Oh, yes, she *wanted* him to taste her. 'Do you think you could kiss me?' she whispered. 'Just for practice?'

Somehow the gap between them seemed to be closing. Gabe was cupping her face with two hands now. He was so close. So wonderfully close. Was he going to kiss her?

She closed her eyes.

'I mustn't kiss you.'

Her eyes flashed open to see him pulling away.

'What was I thinking?' he cried, jumping to his feet.

One glance at the distress in his startled eyes and she felt exceedingly foolish. Embarrassed.

What was wrong with her? What had *she* been thinking? She'd been enjoying his touches so much she'd virtually thrown herself at him. How had she let herself be so carried away? With *Gabe*?

His hands rose to his head in a gesture of helplessness, then they dropped to his side as he let out an angry sound that was half-sigh, half-groan. 'Piper, you have no idea how to protect yourself from men!'

Was he right? Her cheeks flamed as she watched him pace away from her, his boots crunching in the dirt. How on earth had this happened? When had their conversation taken such a dangerous turn? Had it been as Gabe described? Had her senses taken over before her brain could catch up?

He stopped pacing and turned abruptly, and she saw that his face was twisted with fierce emotion. 'For heaven's sake, Piper, if you go around offering yourself like that you'll end up with the wrong man.'

Puzzled, contrite, she stared at him, while she forced her mind back over what had just happened. Minutes ago he'd been gently teasing her, then he'd been touching her with breathtaking tenderness and looking as if he wanted to kiss her as much as she wanted to be kissed. And now he looked more angry and disturbed than she'd ever seen him.

But, hang it all, what did he have to get so fired up about? He'd been the one telling her how pretty her hair looked in the moonlight. He'd raised the subject of intimacy…

Heck! Gabe didn't have a monopoly on anger. She was getting pretty mad, too. She'd been following his lead, trusting him completely while she let her senses take over.

Folding her arms very deliberately across her chest, she glared at him. 'Heaven forbid that I should end up with the wrong man. I wouldn't want a man like you, Gabriel Rivers.'

He didn't reply at first. Just stood there with his hands shoved deeply in his pockets and his jaw set. For ages they stood facing each other without speaking, sizing each other up like gladiators in a ring.

Then Gabe gave a casual shrug of his shoulders and a fleeting grin twisted his mouth. Crossing back towards her, he settled onto the swag again. 'Glad we got that sorted out,' he said.

## CHAPTER THREE

'DID you catch the mongrels?'

Michael Delaney was waiting on the verandah when Gabe and Piper climbed wearily out of the ute shortly after dawn.

'Didn't see hide nor hair of them,' Gabe grumbled.

Piper hurried across the verandah to kiss her grandfather. 'How are you, darling?' She studied him anxiously as she stood holding his frail hand in both of hers. 'Did Roy spend the night here?' she asked.

Roy was an ancient stockman, who was as old and frail as Michael. He'd passed his use-by date as a cattleman years ago, but, unable to face the thought of a retirement home, he'd stayed on in a small cottage on Windaroo and did odd jobs about the place.

'He only slipped back to his cottage a minute ago when he heard your ute coming back,' said Michael.

'How did you sleep?' Piper asked.

'Well enough.'

'And you remembered to take all your tablets?'

Her grandfather sighed. 'Every blinking one of them. I'm so full of pills I'm rattling. Now, forget about me. I want to hear all about your night.'

Gabe caught the sudden tension in Piper as she flicked an annoying strand of hair out of her eyes. This morning she'd been furious when they hadn't been able to find her elastic band. He knew Michael's brain would be computing madly as his shrewd old eyes took in the uncharacteristic wildness of her loose, tousled locks.

In fact, the old man's faded blue eyes were dancing as he swung his gaze from her to Gabe and back again. 'It was a nice night to be out,' he said. 'With the full moon and all it must have been a sweet spring night.'

'It's still August,' Piper huffed. 'Won't be spring until next week.'

Michael ignored her and, settling his frail frame more comfortably in his canvas squatter's chair, smiled smugly.

Gabe wondered why the old fellow was looking so self-satisfied. His own night had been hellishly difficult, and although they hadn't swapped notes, he was sure that Piper hadn't had a wink of sleep either.

Now, for the life of him, he couldn't look cheerful, and when Michael saw no change in Piper's similarly dour expression his smile faltered.

'I was so sure those cattle duffers would hit that paddock last night,' she said. 'I'll be furious if I find out they struck in another spot.' Angrily she shoved her hair behind her ears. 'I dragged Gabe out there for nothing.'

Gabe dropped his gaze in case Michael caught his sudden flush of guilty embarrassment. Thank God *nothing* had happened out there. It had been a close call. Way too close for comfort.

What a fool he'd been to get tangled up in that discussion about flirting. But how could he have known Piper would respond so sensually to his slightest touch?

And how could he have guessed it would be so damn difficult to resist her tempting little mouth? He'd been on the brink of making a huge mistake. And the result had been an uncomfortable tension that had destroyed the easy camaraderie they'd always enjoyed.

'We're disgustingly hungry.' Piper said. 'So I'm going to make breakfast straight away.'

Without looking back at either of them she hurried into the house, and Gabe knew she was itching to get away from him.

'Rest your bones,' Michael ordered, and he patted the flat timber arm of the chair beside him. 'Piper likes to be left alone when she's working in the kitchen.'

Gabe grimaced as he lowered himself slowly into the seat. This morning, after a sleepless night on hard ground, his wounds were complaining. He was aching all over and he felt almost as doddering and brittle as old Michael.

At least he could relax with the old man. They sat in companionable silence for several minutes while they gazed out across Windaroo's pastures.

And then it happened.

Just when he was starting to unwind memories pressed in, demanding his attention, and instead of sunlit, grassy plains he was seeing shattered glass scattering over the highway, buckled metal and his own broken limbs.

If only he could put it all behind him. But more often than he liked memories of the crash still hijacked his thoughts.

He'd heard enough psychobabble to understand why. Suppressed anger was the reason they gave, and it was probably true. His injuries would have been so much easier to accept if they'd happened in the line of duty. Hell, he'd been putting himself in harm's way ever since he joined the army.

Without question he'd gone with the Australian UN

contingent straight into hot-spots like Somalia, Cambodia and Rwanda. He'd come under fire more times than he could count and had had two forced landings that might have been crashes.

But the irony was he'd come through all that unscathed and been wiped out by a speeding semi-trailer on a highway when he was on leave!

*Enough!*

'The country needs rain,' he said, wincing that he'd come up with such a lame topic. But he wanted to find something for Michael to talk about that had nothing to do with Piper.

Michael grunted his agreement, then turned to Gabe. 'Did Piper tell you that I'd spoken to her about—the future?'

'Yes.' Gabe waited a beat before clasping the old man's shoulder. 'I'm sorry to hear such bad news, Michael.'

'It's Piper I'm worried about.'

'She's devastated, of course.'

Michael shot him a piercing glance. 'You know my granddaughter almost as well as I do, Gabe. Do you think she's going to be sensible about everything?'

Gabe hesitated, searching for the best way to answer, but he knew Michael wouldn't appreciate any pussy-footing around the truth. 'I'm sure you realise she's pretty cut up that you want to sell Windaroo.'

'Yeah, I know.' Michael sighed loudly. 'But you can understand why I have to, can't you, boy? I couldn't go to my grave knowing she's been left saddled with this place. It's been getting run down in recent years. There are debts. It would be a huge burden.'

'Well...I should warn you that she's planning to outfox you. She's determined to find a way to stay here.'

To Gabe's surprise Michael didn't look as put out by this news as he'd expected.

'She is, is she?' he said slowly, and a little of the old sparkle flashed in his eyes. 'Did she happen to tell you what she has in mind?'

Gabe wasn't a man to betray a confidence, but Piper had been quite open about her plans. And for some reason he liked the idea of having Michael in the know. The old fellow could vet Piper's line-up of suitors. 'She plans to find herself a husband,' he said.

Michael slapped his thigh gleefully. 'Well, bully for her.' He winked at Gabe. 'She told you this last night, did she?'

Gabe nodded, not at all happy with the shining smile on his old friend's whiskery face.

'And?' Michael prompted eagerly.

'And what?'

'And what did you decide to do about it?'

Gabe's insides took a tumble-turn. 'What did *I* decide?'

'You heard me.'

'Steady on, old mate. It's got nothing to do with me.'

'Hurrumph!' Michael drooped as if he'd been physically wounded and made no effort to hide his disgust.

'Hey,' Gabe cried, leaning forward and shaking Michael's arm gently. 'You romantic old fool. You couldn't possibly have thought I'd propose to her, could you?'

'Stranger things have happened,' came the sulky reply. 'Besides, I know how you feel about her.'

The words seemed to explode in Gabe's face. It was

like the crash all over again. He couldn't feel his limbs. He was fighting for breath.

*I know how you feel about her…* What the hell did that mean? The old man was deluding himself. How could Michael know what Gabe himself didn't know? How was he *supposed* to feel about Piper?

She was the kid next door. She was special, sure. Gutsy, vibrant, doggedly loyal. He'd always admired her sweet, unaffected nature and her spirit of adventure. He felt a strong bond with her—a sense of responsibility towards her. No doubt about it. But beyond that?

His stomach took a plunge.

No way… The close call with that kiss last night was nothing. It had been an aberration…nothing more. *Nothing.*

Michael was watching him with the wary attention of a man in the dock awaiting the jury's verdict.

What the hell did the old fellow expect? Gabe was years older than Piper. Right now he felt as old as Methuselah. He had an uncertain future to sort out. And the stark reality was that he was a damaged man. Even if he wanted to—and he couldn't honestly say that he did—he couldn't think twice about shackling himself to a vibrant young woman like Piper.

'Piper has her sights set on someone much younger and fitter than I am,' he told Michael.

For an embarrassingly long minute Michael stared at him in disbelief. Then a kind of acceptance seemed to settle in his tired old eyes. 'Who is he?' His smile was conspiratorial. 'We can find out where he drinks and sort him out.'

Gabe laughed. 'I don't think she has an actual candidate lined up just yet.'

'Ah!' The tension left the old man. He relaxed back into his chair, folded his hands in his lap and smiled contentedly into the distance.

'But she's going to start seriously hunting for a husband,' Gabe added as a warning.

'Let her hunt,' came the unexpected reply.

Gabe frowned. 'I should warn you that she's looking for a husband in the hope that it will stop you from selling Windaroo.'

'She's dead right,' he responded brightly. 'I wouldn't need to sell this place if she had the right man to help her run it.'

'So you'd be quite happy to see her throw herself on the marriage market?'

Michael eyed him shrewdly. 'Don't you think it's a good idea?'

Gabe shifted uneasily beneath the faded blue gaze. 'I wouldn't know what's best for her. I'm not her grandfather.'

Leaning closer, Michael touched him on the arm so that he had to turn back, and when he did the old fellow winked. 'I reckon there's no harm in letting her look around. It'll help her to see the lie of the land. Right now she can't see the wood for the trees.' He winked at Gabe. 'You'll keep an eye on her, won't you, son?'

'Surely you don't want me snooping around like some kind of private eye?'

Michael lifted his shoulders in a helpless little shrug. 'She's a babe in the woods. There are wolves out there.'

'I'll cramp her style.'

But Michael had a trump card up his sleeve. 'I'm a dying old man. Can't you do this for me?'

Gabe's eyes narrowed. He'd never realised Michael Delaney was such a crafty old beggar.

'You'll promise me this one thing, won't you, boy?'

Gabe sighed. 'I don't know how long I'm going to be in the district—but OK, it's a deal.' Then he shot to his feet.

'Something smells good,' Michael said. 'I'm sure our breakfast's ready.'

But the conversation had curbed Gabe's appetite. 'I need to get back home,' he said. 'Jonno's expecting me to give him a hand with some stockyard work today.'

In the kitchen, Piper was carrying toast and butter to the table when she caught sight of her reflection in a battered old mirror that hung near the hat pegs. She gasped at the sight of herself with her hair all wild and loose around her face like a silky halo.

With hardly a thought to where she dumped the toast, she drifted closer to the mirror. How different she looked. For a moment she forgot the embarrassment of her foolish behaviour last night. She was thinking instead of the gentle, caressing way Gabe had threaded his fingers through her hair and the way he'd stroked her skin.

A tide of pink rose from her neck to her cheeks and she looked happy and rosy. Almost glowing—like a computer-enhanced picture in a glossy magazine.

Idiot!

She had nothing to make her smile. Nothing to go all vain and gooey about. How could she have been so stupid as to ask Gabe to kiss her? Gabe, who'd been kissed and seduced by squillions of sexy women.

She swung away from the mirror. Last night had

merely reinforced what she already knew. She had a long way to go before she worked out the finer points of catching a man.

Hurrying into the bathroom, she grabbed her hairbrush and set about flattening her hair, then pulled it back tightly with another elasticised band.

One thing was certain. Next time she practised flirting she'd make sure Gabe Rivers was nowhere near.

## CHAPTER FOUR

'It's not me. I'm not this sophisticated. I feel strange.' Piper stood in her grandfather's bedroom and stared at her reflection in the full-length mirror. What she saw was beyond anything she could have imagined.

'You look fantastic, darlin',' Michael reassured her from the doorway. His smile was so bright it would have glowed in the dark. 'You look like a princess.'

'You don't think I've gone too far? I'm showing so much bare skin.'

'Nonsense. Anyway, your skin's lovely. It should be seen. You'll knock 'em dead tonight.'

She turned sideways to check her gown from a different angle and told herself it was too late to back out now; she'd taken the bull by the horns. She was going to the Mullinjim Spring Ball to start her husband-hunt. In earnest.

Knowing she desperately needed help in matters of make-up, hairstyles and ballgowns, she'd followed up an advertisement in the local paper and hired the services of a travelling beauty and grooming consultant. The whole process had been a steep learning curve!

April, the consultant, had been quite definite.

'White,' she said. 'The dark vamp look is so last century. You should certainly wear white. It's dramatic and it's classy and you have the perfect youthful complexion for it. Not everyone can wear white successfully, you know.'

It crossed Piper's mind that a white gown would

scream virgin to the entire population, but she held her tongue.

'And you're slim and fit, so a tight, low-necked, low-backed gown will be best, to show off your figure and that beautiful pale skin,' April continued with growing enthusiasm. 'And your shoulders are so nicely defined you'll only want the tiniest halterneck strap to hold everything up.'

'What about...?' With a grimace, Piper indicated her inadequacies in the chest department.

'You wait till you see the dress I have in mind. Your curves will be shown off to their best advantage,' April reassured her, and then she winked. 'At least you should be grateful you have firm breasts that haven't started heading south yet. Most women have the opposite problem.'

So the dress had been couriered out from a Cairns boutique, and this afternoon April had attended to the final details of hair and make-up.

'You need after-dark glamour to bring out your eyes. They're a pretty blue, but they could look a bit quiet at night, so I'll apply shadow to define them. And then we'll add false eyelashes.'

'Oh, no, we won't!' Piper knew when enough was enough. 'I couldn't possibly wear false eyelashes.'

'You wait till you see the way I do it, ducks. I'm a genius. I cut them and just apply a few extra lashes to your outer lid. It gives you a sexy, long-lash look, but I promise you won't look like a drag queen.'

Pushing a host of doubts aside, Piper had bravely submitted to the superior knowledge of an expert. Now, as she viewed the results, she had to agree that April was indeed a genius. A very expensive genius, but she was definitely up there with fairy godmothers when it came to transforming tomboys into princesses.

The white gown was a silken dream. It seemed to give Piper's body a sexy allure she'd never imagined possible. She'd expected to leave her hair down, the way Gabe had suggested, but April had done it in an elegant twist— 'To show off your neck and shoulders.'

Her face looked amazing. She'd been worried that her eyes would look overly painted, but April's artwork was subtle. She turned away from the mirror to see Michael regarding her tenderly.

'I have one last thing that will add the finishing touch to make you look beyond perfect,' he told her as he stood there with his hands behind his back.

'What is it?'

With a little boy's look-at-me-Mum smile, he brought his hands forward. 'These were Bella's.'

Piper's heartbeats quickened. Michael had never before shown her anything that had belonged to her mother apart from photos. Now, sitting in the palm of his old callused hand, she saw elegant earrings—beautiful teardrop pearls suspended from tiny circles of diamonds.

'Oh, Grandad, they're gorgeous.' She threw her arms around him, and the only thing that stopped her from crying was fear that her make-up would run. 'Thank you,' she whispered. 'I never knew my mother had such lovely things. But I don't suppose she was ever a rough and tumble tomboy like me.'

'Oh, Bella was a tomboy all right,' Michael said with a wistful smile. 'Right up until the day Peter O'Malley arrived in our valley and swept her off her feet. Suddenly there was a flurry of buying dresses and fixing hair and you would have been pushed to recognise her. She turned from a sunburnt and dusty jillaroo into a beautiful princess overnight.'

Piper felt a twisting ache around her heart as she thought about her parents falling in love. Her glance darted to her reflection in the mirror.

'Yes. You look just as suddenly grown-up and pretty as she did, sweetheart. I've always known that you'd steal hearts one day. Your sweet blue eyes are exactly like Bella's and you have a beautiful, proud profile like my Mary's...and your father's yellow hair.'

He cupped his hand and tipped it from side to side so that the earrings caught the light and the diamonds sparkled. 'Peter bought these for Bella to wear on her wedding day. They were married right here at Windaroo, under the jacaranda tree next to the front steps. It was the prettiest wedding you could ever imagine.'

'Oh, Grandad, don't make me cry.'

'Sorry, Piper. I guess seeing you looking so lovely made me nostalgic.' As he handed her the earrings he grinned. 'I should warn you that I have a hankering to see another wedding on Windaroo some time soon.'

'Don't get your hopes up, old feller,' she said, shooting him a warning glance.

He chuckled, and then, as if to change the subject, said, 'Hey, that's nice man-bait you're wearing.'

'Man-bait?'

'Perfume.'

She turned away quickly and slipped the first earring in. 'Do you think the scent is delicate enough?'

'It smells better than bread in the oven.'

'That's very reassuring.' She laughed and finished securing the second earring. Another glance in the mirror told her they were the perfect touch of elegance. 'What do you think?' she asked, turning back to him.

The old man's eyes gleamed as he saw the jewellery in place. 'You're going to capture a whole battalion of hearts tonight, little girl.'

Arm in arm they walked out to the verandah.

Old Roy, who was keeping Michael company this evening, was there sitting in a squatter's chair, and he jumped to his feet when he saw them. 'Holy smoke!' He stared at Piper.

Michael beamed at him. 'What do you think of our princess?'

Roy ran his hand over his bald patch several times. 'Holy smoke,' he said again. 'Strike me pink. Piper—geez, you look a bit of all right.'

'Thanks, Roy,' Piper said with a smile. What would she do without these two old darlings? They were certainly good for a girl's ego.

She and Michael walked on to the ute, parked in the driveway. As he opened the door for her he patted the battered frame. 'You should be heading off in a golden coach with six white horses, not this old rattletrap.'

With an exaggerated roll of her eyes she climbed behind the steering wheel and tossed her evening purse onto the passenger's seat.

'At any rate you should have a partner to take you to this ball,' Michael added. 'I'm not happy at the idea of you going by yourself. It's not how we did things in my day.'

'I'm safe to drive. I'll limit myself to one glass of wine.' She frowned at him. 'Now, don't you dare spend your night worrying about me.' The doctor's warning that his heart couldn't take any more attacks hung over her like the sword of Damocles.

'I'm not going to worry. Just the same, I wish you'd asked Gabe to take you to this ball.'

Piper released a weary sigh. Over the past fortnight they'd seen very little of Gabe, but he'd come into her grandfather's conversations far too often. 'You know jolly well that I'm trying to find a husband. Gabe would only get in the way.'

'You reckon?' he asked, looking crestfallen.

'I'm sure of it.'

The old man dropped his gaze and shook his head slowly. Then his eyes sought hers again. 'About this husband-hunt of yours…'

'Yes?'

'I know what's driving you to do this, Piper, and I feel responsible, so I'd like to offer you a word of advice.'

Her heart gave a strange little jump. 'What is it?'

'You might think I'm just an old romantic fool,' he said, 'but no matter how eager you are to get yourself hitched, you should listen to your heart when you choose your husband, not your head.'

'You are a romantic old fool,' she told him. 'But I love you and I'll try to remember your advice.'

Leaning through the ute's window, she blew him a kiss, then she accelerated down the drive. Tears threatened again as she watched him through her rear-vision mirror. He was standing at the foot of Windaroo's steps, watching her with that dear smile of his, and the thought that one day he wouldn't be there was unbearable.

She tried to cheer herself up by thinking of the exciting night ahead, and wondered why she didn't feel more uplifted by the thought that Gabe wouldn't be at the ball to see her all dolled up like this.

The Mullinjim Spring Ball was held in the Community Hall—a simple weatherboard building. Tonight its interior was decorated with potted palms, streamers, balloons and crêpe paper flowers. At one end of the hall a four-piece band was squeezed onto a tiny stage, and in the kitchen area, where the Country Women's Association usually served tea and scones, the Social Committee had set up a makeshift bar.

In true outback style, the people of the surrounding districts overlooked the venue's lack of sophistication and dressed as grandly as they would if they were attending the Sydney Opera House. The men wore stylish black dinner suits and the women were in long, formal gowns in a rainbow of pretty colours.

When Piper arrived she headed straight for the ringers and graziers she'd known all her life—the guys she'd always hung out with at parties until they found a girl they fancied. Tonight they were gathered around the bar.

It wasn't till she was halfway across the hall that nerves struck. Suddenly the full impact of the task ahead hit her and almost sent her turning back and scampering off into the night. Oh, man! Tonight she had to tackle some serious flirting.

If only she'd watched more romance movies instead of cowboy flicks. Right now she would have felt more at ease sauntering into a western saloon full of mean-eyed baddies in black cowboy hats than facing this innocuous collection of cattlemen in dinner suits.

They might be husband material, but they were still blissfully unaware of their possible fate, and somehow she had to convince them to start thinking of her—tomboy Piper O'Malley—as a potential wife!

Yikes! Her knees were going on her. *Get over this and start flirting!* What was it Gabe had told her? Flirting and flattery go hand in hand.

OK.

Her palms were very damp as she ran them down her silk-covered thighs and she hoped they didn't leave a snail trail. *It's like swimming in a freezing cold creek. You've just got to dive in.*

*Go!*

Taking a deep breath, she flashed a bright smile and stepped closer to the bar. 'Hi, dudes,' she said. 'You're all looking very swish.'

Several heads turned her way.

Turned casually and then jerked to attention.

Mouths fell open. Eyes popped.

Jock Fleming from Jupiter Downs spilled his beer.

'Blow me down,' Steve Flaxton said at last. 'Is it Piper?'

'Of course it's me!' Panic exploded like a shotgun blast in her chest. 'What's the matter? What are you staring at?'

What had she done wrong? Left a zip undone? Was an eyelash dangling? Surely she hadn't popped out of the top of her dress?

'Is it my hair?' she cried, her eyes frantically searching for a mirror. 'What's wrong with me?'

Jonno Rivers, Gabe's brother, found his tongue first. 'Sorry, Piper. It's just we've never seen you looking like this.'

'So?' she cried. They were still staring at her as if they'd been frozen in shock mode. But her initial panic gave way to a flash of relief, quickly followed by anger. Fury. Disappointment! Surely these guys could do better than to stand there and gape like stupefied dolts?

Where were their admiring smiles? Their gallant gestures? One of these fools was supposed to sweep her off her feet and become her romantic soul mate.

Couldn't one of them, at the very least, offer to get her a drink?

'What's wrong with you mob? Don't you know how to treat a woman?'

Behind her, the band struck up a lively number and people began to move onto the dance floor. Jock, Steve, Jonno and the others looked nervously at one another. To her right, she heard some oaf mutter, 'Since when has Piper had tits? Where's she been hiding them?'

She whirled towards the voice. But before she could find words to make the toad squirm, she was aware of gazes shifting past her to the hall's entrance, and she turned to see a tall, dark and commanding figure.

Gabe.

Oh, help.

He was standing in the doorway on the far side of the hall and she had the distinct impression he'd been watching them. Oh, Lord! Her insides seemed to collapse. *Nosy* Gabe!

He was the last person she wanted to witness this humiliation. He wasn't supposed to be here! How could she relax enough to flirt successfully while her tutor watched from the sidelines?

She had to admit he looked magnificent. Every man in the room was dressed in a tuxedo like his, but no one else looked so darkly handsome, so silently strong and significant. He strode into the room with his shoulders squared and his eyes narrowed. Heads turned. Most of the people present watched his entry and Piper could understand why. He looked every inch a—a hero.

But of course he *was* a hero!

Before his accident he'd flown into the face of death, braved treacherous cyclones to rescue yachtsmen drowning at sea. He'd defied raging bushfires to save families from hellish flames and in Timor he'd rescued refugees as they were chased by machete-wielding militia.

She comforted herself with the thought that a man who'd done all that wouldn't gape like a village idiot just because a girl had put on a dress and fixed her hair in a fancy twist.

Just the same, an embarrassing warmth crept up her neck and into her cheeks as he continued across the room. Any minute now he would reach her. What would he think of the way she looked?

One thing was certain. He'd take a contemptuous look at these fools around her, sum up the situation and, in true hero-style, recognise that the lady needed rescuing.

He'd ask her to dance.

Gulp. The thought of dancing with Gabe didn't do much to calm her jumping nerves. Being in his arms, having him so near... It might make them both remember the embarrassment of that night when she'd asked him to kiss her. And what if she felt like that again? As if she was a string of fire crackers and he was a lighted match!

Could she cope?

She *had* to. She needed to be rescued from these simpletons. She would most definitely cope.

He drew closer.

And the annoying electricity started again. Heat sparked and spread under her skin. His dark, unsmiling gaze settled on her and her breathing went haywire as his smouldering eyes took in every detail of her appearance. Travelled all over her like a trembling heat haze...over her hair...her neck and shoulders...her softly clinging gown...

*What did he think?*

His eyes locked with hers and his expression was stern and sad and somehow…lost.

She forced a tiny smile.

The answering movement of his facial muscles wasn't a smile.

*Don't look at me like that. Please, Gabe, I need you to save me.*

He stepped closer and nodded. 'Evening, Piper.' There was still no smile, and without another word his eyes left her.

*What?* He couldn't let her down. Not Gabe. But he was turning his attention to the half-circle of men gathered along the bar.

'Steve,' he said, 'where are your manners?'

'What are you talking about?' Steve Flaxton cried.

'Ask the lady to dance.'

There was deathly silence along the bar as Steve and Piper both stared at Gabe. She was trembling. This didn't make sense. How could Gabe, who had never let her down, be so insensitive now, when she needed him most?

He stood stiffly to attention, leaving no doubt that when he issued an order he expected to be obeyed.

Far too many painful seconds passed before Steve set his glass on the bar and smiled awkwardly at Piper. 'How about it?' he asked, cocking his head towards the dance floor.

The last thing she wanted was to dance in front of this crowd. Not now. Not in high heels when her knees were liquid. But, damn Gabe's eyes, she wasn't going to let him see how he'd unnerved her.

'Thank you, Steve,' she whispered and, tight smile in place, placed her evening bag on the bar beside Jonno and turned towards the circling dancers without looking at Gabe.

Hero? *Huh!*

Poor Steve wasn't very good at dancing, but they managed to move around the floor together, copying the moves of the others.

'Quite a crowd here,' he said, after he'd apologised for stepping on her toes for the third time.

'It's great to see such a turn-out.'

'Where'd you learn to dance, Piper?'

'Boarding school.'

They made another awkward but moderately successful circuit of the dance floor. 'Steve,' Piper asked, unable to hold back any longer, 'do you think I look too overdone?'

'Course not,' he said, staring straight at her chest. 'You look great.'

'So what's wrong with the guys? Why are they behaving as if I've just announced I have every contagious disease known to medical science?'

'It's just we've never seen you looking like this.'

'Looking like a female?'

'Yeah,' he said, eyes still focused on her low neckline. 'It's a bit of a shock. But, honestly, you look great. Bloody fantastic.'

'Well, thanks—I think. But I never realised that dressing like a woman would mean men would start talking to my chest instead of to my face.'

Steve flushed bright red.

And Piper felt terrible.

What a joke to think she'd been going to find a husband among this lot! As if doing the Cinderella act with a new gown and hairstyle would automatically change one of these country boys into Prince Charming.

She'd known them all her life and she'd never once been attracted to any of them. As a young teenager she'd avoided their clumsy attempts to kiss her and she was no more interested now.

Over Steve's shoulder, she surveyed the hall. How was she going to hang around this ball for the rest of the night? It would be slow torture. She didn't have a close girlfriend her age to confide in. Most of the young women who'd stayed in the district had married very young and had drifted out of her social circle, but she supposed she could chat to them and help them to keep their youngsters from getting under the dancers' feet.

As for the young, single women, she hardly knew any of them. Most of them had come from the city—teachers, nurses or public servants doing their stint of country service in Mullinjim or other towns in the valley. They knew everything about clothes and make-up. Had probably learned it before they were out of nappies. They certainly hadn't needed a grooming consultant to help them look so chic and trendy. Or super-confident.

And they had all known to come to the ball with partners.

So she was stuck with her usual social group—the blokes around the bar. And what a dead loss they were.

That left Gabe.

And he'd made her feel the size of a split atom. After issuing his order to Steve he'd sauntered away to have a drink and convivial conversation with the superintendent of the hospital and his wife.

As far as her husband-hunt was concerned, the Mullinjim Spring Ball was a wipe out.

The dance bracket came to an end and Steve looked as relieved as she felt. 'Thank you. That was lovely,' she said.

Steve was about to dash away when he remembered his manners. 'Would you like a drink?'

A drink meant going back to the bar and a dozen pairs of eyes staring at her chest. 'No, but you go join the others. If you could just fetch my bag, I'd like to get some fresh air.'

As soon as Steve delivered her purse Piper hurried to the doorway and slipped outside, where it was refreshingly dark and cool. She wanted to fling herself onto one of the old wooden seats, but she was afraid of getting splinters in her dress, so she stood with her hands behind her back and drew in a deep breath of night air—clean, country air faintly scented by wisteria.

She wouldn't go back inside. The band, the bright lights and the strain of it all had given her a humdinger of a headache.

Crossing the footpath to the vacant lot where she'd left her ute, she knew she couldn't go home yet either. Her grandfather would be devastated if she came home early. But she could visit Nellie Davies, an elderly friend of her grandfather's who lived in a cottage next to the post office. Kicking off her fancy shoes and having a cup of tea with Nellie sounded good. It would help her headache. Perhaps she could even confide in Nellie about her disappointing evening.

She set out across the gravel car park, walking gingerly in her high heels.

Out of the corner of his eye, Gabe spied the slender white shape slipping out through the doorway. 'Excuse me,' he said to Dr Springer and his wife. 'I need to catch someone before—she—I mean he—leaves.'

Jim Springer, who'd noticed the direction of Gabe's

gaze, smiled knowingly. 'Don't let us hold you up, old chap. She—I mean he—looked in a bit of a hurry.'

Outside, Piper's white dress was easy to spot. She was halfway across the vacant lot that served as a car park before he was close enough to call to her.

When he did she turned, and his chest tightened. What a thickhead he was! He'd rushed out here with no particular reason. Why the hell had he charged after her? 'Where are you going?' he asked, feeling foolish.

'It's none of your business,' she said with her chin high, and he had to admit she was absolutely right. She swung away from him once more and continued on towards her ute.

Lunging forward, Gabe gripped her elbow. She froze. When their eyes met, hers were challenging. She looked ready for a fight.

But she looked lovely too. Impossibly lovely. Was this really the same little Piper who'd asked his advice? Thank heavens she hadn't listened. He'd told her to leave her hair down, but the way it was now, gathered in a golden knot high on her head, was enchanting. It left the delicate curve of her neck exposed. Such a slender white neck.

And her shoulders. Heavens, who could have guessed they would be so perfect? As for her arms…so much pale, soft skin. Such bewitching curves…

And her painted lips looked so glamorous and grown-up.

'Gabe, let me go.'

He blinked. 'You're not running away, are you?' he asked, remembering why he was holding her.

'What if I am?'

'But—but you've only just arrived. The evening's

hardly started. You can't launch a husband-hunt from the car park.'

She shrugged her elbow out of his grasp. 'I'm not going to find a husband here. This ball is a waste of time.'

'You've decided that already?'

'Those guys in there can't get past looking at me as if I'm a bloke who's had a sudden sex change.'

He couldn't help grinning.

But Piper seemed to have lost her sense of humour. 'You can smirk, Gabe, but you embarrassed me in there just as much as they did. You're nothing but a big bully. How do you think I felt when you started ordering people to dance with me like you're still in the army and I'm some kind of military mission?'

'You're exaggerating, Piper. Those silly fellows needed someone to wake them up. But, listen, you mustn't run away.'

'I *mustn't*? Is this another order?'

'Of course not. But you can't waste all this.' Lord help him. He couldn't resist touching her dress. Just the briefest glide of his hand from her slender waist to her silken hip. 'You look beautiful.'

'Beautiful?' she echoed in a choky little voice.

He could tell that she wanted to believe him. Needed to believe him. He reached for her again, and as he gripped her arms she didn't pull away. 'I mean it, Piper. You look so incredibly beautiful you've knocked everyone for six.'

She bit her lower lip and looked away. 'Fat lot of good it did me.'

'You've got to give those blokes a bit more time,' he said. 'They'll snap out of their shock if you just give them a chance to come up for air. After a few more dances they'll be fighting to take you home.'

'Well, there's a problem,' she said, stiffening her shoulders.

'What's that?'

'I don't want to go home with any of them.'

Her answer sent a weird, light-hearted fizz rushing through Gabe. A stupid and unreasonable reaction. He shoved the feeling aside. 'So you went to all this trouble and now you're not going to give them a chance?'

'I'm twenty-three years old, Gabe. I've known most of these fellows since they were five or six. How many chances do they need?'

His hands dropped away from her and they stood facing each other.

Her chin tilted haughtily. 'I've learned one very good lesson tonight.'

'Which is?'

Her lips compressed, as if she didn't want to tell him, and Gabe couldn't for the life of him work out why her answer seemed so damned important.

Her gaze dropped to her hands as they twisted the clasp of her small evening bag. 'I'm not going to find a husband around here,' she said at last. 'I need to look outside this town.'

He didn't reply at first—just stood watching her for several seconds. 'So you'll head for the city?'

'How can I? I can't leave Grandad. I'm just going to have to—' Before she could finish her answer, headlights swept over them and gravel crunched as a car came into the car park. It pulled in beside them.

'Hi, Gabe.' A neighbour, Joe Hutchins, called out. He peered through the side window at Piper and nodded as he might to someone he didn't know, then looked again, harder. 'Is that Piper?' he asked.

'Hi, Joe.'

'Geez. Didn't recognise you. Hey, listen, I don't want to alarm you, but on the way through I saw a cattle truck with a couple of trail bikes on the back. They turned off on the Sandy Creek Road. Looked like they could be heading for Windaroo.'

'Oh, God. It'll be those cattle duffers again.' She shot a glance skywards. 'But why tonight? It's a new moon—not much light at all.'

'They're damn sneaky barstools,' said Joe. 'Makes sense for them to choose a night when most people are out kicking up their heels and enjoying themselves.'

'Including the boys from our local Police Stock Squad,' added Gabe. He looked towards the hall. 'Thanks for the warning, Joe. I'll go in and have a quick word with the guys inside, but I don't suppose they'll be interested in doing much tonight, especially as we only have suspicions with no hard evidence.'

As soon as Joe drove out of the car park and Gabe had headed back into the hall Piper picked up her skirt and dashed towards her ute. There was no time to waste. Gabe was right. The Stock Squad boys wouldn't be too happy about being dragged away from their night off at the ball.

And most of the young men had already downed several beers, so they wouldn't be much use. If she told them about the thieves they'd almost certainly offer to come and help, but the last thing she needed was a bunch of fellows half full of grog, stumbling around in the scrub and making too much noise.

No, if she wanted to get a close look at these thieves she would have to get out to Sandy Creek on her own.

What sneaky creeps these cattle duffers were. No doubt they'd been targeting Windaroo because they thought a sick old man and a young girl wouldn't stand up to them. Well, she'd show them!

Her ballgown was hardly suitable for sneaking around in the bush, but as she always kept a spare set of old working clothes in the back of the ute it wasn't a problem. However, the question of where to change *was*.

She balked at the idea of going back into the hall. All those eyes would be watching her again. And she would have to waste time explaining to all and sundry why she'd abandoned her ballgown to change into old jeans, a work shirt and boots.

No, it would be much better to get changed out here. In the dark, behind the ute.

Before Gabe came back.

The elegant shoes went first. She tossed them into the ute. Next, she hitched her skirt high, undid her stockings and rolled them quickly downwards. She'd actually been enjoying the unaccustomed luxury of super-fine, silky stockings, but too bad. They and her suspender belt followed the shoes into the cabin of the ute.

Next came the dress. Crouching low in the shadows, she slid the zip down and managed to wriggle out of the slim white sheath. She felt a flash of regret to be shedding so much glamour so quickly, but there was no time to be sentimental. Pushing the gown through the window onto the passenger's seat, she told herself she would find somewhere safe to stow it later.

Now, where were her jeans?

It was so difficult to see in the dark. The back of the old ute held a tangle of ropes, fencing wire, tools and old motor parts. And somewhere in there were her clothes. Once upon a time they had been in a cardboard box, but after rattling around on outback roads for several weeks, everything had been shaken up.

Finally her fingers closed around denim. Thank goodness. She hauled the jeans out. But now she couldn't see in the dark to sort out which leg went where. She had no choice but to move a little towards the light cast by a street lamp.

'What the hell are you doing?'

Gabe's voice came out of nowhere.

# CHAPTER FIVE

'WHAT are *you* doing here?' Piper spun around, frantically trying to tug her jeans up her legs as she did so. Why hadn't she heard Gabe's footsteps?

'I asked first.'

He was standing at the end of the ute. The glow of the street light showed her the slow, teasing gleam in his eyes and the smile lurking at the corners of his mouth. He stood with one nonchalant elbow propped on the tailgate.

'Turn around,' she snapped as, with a final desperate tug, she hauled her jeans into place. 'Where are your manners, Gabe?

'I wasn't checking you out,' he drawled. 'Well…not for *very* long.' He turned his back to her slowly. Way too slowly.

*The rat!*

Cheeks flaming, heart racing, she groped wildly in the back of the ute for her shirt.

Gabe spoke over his shoulder in an annoyingly slow, amused drawl. 'You've nothing to worry about, Piper. At least you're wearing your best underwear.'

'Go take a flying leap!'

Damn the man. He was supposed to be a gentleman. She didn't need his amused reminder that he'd had an eyeful of her underwear. Her incredibly expensive, designer label underwear. Yikes! The wispy white satin and lace uplift bra left little to the imagination, and as for the hardly-there panties April had insisted she needed under the slinky gown…! Her brain would short-circuit if she thought about how much they revealed!

*Where the heck was her shirt?* She died a thousand deaths as she groped in panicky haste among the tools and wire, cursing the fact that she'd been too addle-headed to find the clothes first, *before* she started undressing.

'Gabe,' she called, after painful minutes of fruitless searching, her voice sounding squeaky and pathetic, as if she'd rather disappear through a never-ending hole in the universe than ask this question. 'Could you have a look down your end and see if you can find my shirt?'

'With pleasure, ma'am.'

He turned and she saw straight away that he was still smiling. How dared he enjoy himself at her expense? She hated him!

'Is this what you're looking for?' He waved her blue and white check shirt above his head like a flag.

'Throw it here.'

'Come and get it,' he teased.

Her hands flew to cover her chest. 'I don't have time to waste playing games.'

'Spoilsport.' With an exaggerated sigh, Gabe sent the shirt sailing through the air. She caught it and rammed her arms into the sleeves so quickly she heard a seam tear. Too bad. She wrenched the driver's door open.

He was at her side before she could pull the door behind her. 'Don't forget these, Cinderella.' Her riding boots were dangling from two of his fingers.

'Thanks,' she muttered ungraciously.

'Now, you'd better answer my question,' he said,

holding her door firmly open. 'What do you think you're doing?'

'It's obvious, isn't it? I'm going out to Sandy Creek.'

'Not on your own, you're not. I'll come with you.'

'No—' She tried to object, but her protest lost its bite as a sensible voice in her head whispered that she could do with some back-up on this. Besides, Gabe didn't wait for her answer. Before she'd finished hauling her boots on he'd circled the ute and opened the passenger's door.

Her gown was lying on the seat and, despite the car park's gloom, it shimmered like a little lake of woven moonbeams.

'Don't squash that!' she cried.

'Wouldn't dream of it.' With surprising care he lifted the silk garment, then picked up her suspender belt and held it between forefinger and thumb.

'Give that here.' Grabbing it from him, she shoved it and her stockings into the glove box.

Gabe lowered himself onto the seat and settled the dress on his lap. The sight of her white silky dress in his hands sent a strange shiver through her, turning her arms to goosebumps. The garment looked so undeniably feminine against the solid, masculine black of his formal trousers.

The clothes of a bride and groom.

*Crikey!* What was the matter with her? She'd had a close encounter of the undressed kind and her feeble mind had galloped off on a wild tangent!

A wave of anger swept through her. How could she have drippy feelings at a time like this? She was furious with herself. And mad with Gabe! Incensed that every one of her efforts to make a success of this evening had been a failure.

The expensive dress, the hair and the make-up had all been wasted. Gabe, the sergeant-major, had made everything worse at the ball, and then he'd behaved like a creep in the car park. And now cattle duffers were stealing her cattle!

Men! All of her problems were male. Why on earth would she want to get married?

She gunned the ignition and the ute kangaroo-hopped forward before stalling. Blast! She was so flustered she'd forgotten to put the gearstick into neutral first. Talk about embarrassing! She'd been driving since she was big enough to see over the steering wheel and she hadn't done anything so stupid for at least a decade!

She flashed a scowl that she hoped would silence the ace pilot at her side. It didn't.

'There's no need to hurry,' he said with annoying calm.

'Of course there is.'

Once more she started the motor, and this time reversed smoothly out of the parking space.

'Have you thought about what you're letting yourself in for, chasing off after these guys?' he asked.

'I'm protecting my cattle, of course.'

'Don't forget that with current beef prices and the rising penalties for duffing there's every chance a thief caught in the act might rather shoot than risk a jail sentence.'

Piper gave a so-what shrug.

'We should be satisfied with trying to get a look at them,' he continued. 'Or at the registration numbers on their vehicles. After that we can report what we find to the Stock Squad and let them deal with it from there.'

She let out a little huff of annoyance. It was all very

well for Gabe to lecture her, but he'd never cared about the cattle industry the way she had. *She* was the one who'd been working cattle for the past ten years. And these were *her* cattle at risk.

As she turned onto the main road she hitched her chin to a stubborn angle. 'I want to catch these duffers red-handed.'

'But there could be two, maybe three armed men out there.'

'We can sneak up on them, can't we?'

He treated her to a long, sceptical frown. 'Like in a Hollywood movie?'

'Why not?'

'You mean you're going to distract the ring leader so I can deck him with one punch?'

'Yeah, of course. And then the other two might try to jump you, but you'll take a swipe at one of them and he'll bite the dust, and the third will try to escape, but you'll crash-tackle him, and I'll be standing by with my ropes ready to tie them up.'

Gabe sent her a stiff grin. 'An ambitious little project for a shrimp of a girl and a guy with a busted leg.'

She knew he wanted her to return the smile, to acknowledge that they'd both been joking, that she really was going to be sensible tonight. But that felt too much like giving in to Gabe, letting him regain control. She wasn't ready for that. She was still too angry!

And her anger hadn't died by the time they were bouncing along the Sandy Creek Road, which was little more than a bumpy, rutted track.

'Slow down, Piper.'

'I'm not speeding.'

Gabe's eyes narrowed as he watched the twin headlights of a vehicle flickering towards them through the trees, and he didn't bother to suppress an impatient growl. Rocketing along this track in the dark was bad enough, without the added threat of oncoming traffic. 'Take a look at those lights ahead. There's a big vehicle approaching. I'd say it could be the cattle truck.'

'They'd have to be mighty fast workers to have grabbed the cattle and be making their getaway already.'

'They're probably experienced stockmen. If they were well organised they could've cleared a paddock and be making their escape by now.'

She thrust her chin over the steering wheel and peered stubbornly through the dusty windscreen. 'Whoever they are, they're hogging the road.' Puffing out her lips, she made an irritated, blowing sound. 'Surely they can see us. I'm driving with the lights on high beam and I've got the spotlight on as well.'

Gabe leaned towards her and checked the speedometer. 'Those blokes are coming straight on. *Slow down!*'

'If they have Windaroo cattle in the back of that truck I'm not going to let them get past me.'

'Don't be stupid!'

Gabe's heart began to pump harder. Sweat broke out on his brow and he saw his accident again in ghastly, gruesome detail. The horror of metal screeching…glass shattering…his car disintegrating all around him…then silence…and the cold, menacing shadow of death closing in around his mangled body.

'We've got these mongrels cornered. I won't let them past.'

'You're crazy!' He tried to fight off more visions of another collision—frightening scenes of Piper's ute wrecked and shoved aside by the big cattle truck—Piper, bleeding and injured. Dead. 'They're speeding up and they're three times our weight!' he shouted. 'Slow down, for God's sake! Pull off the road! Piper, this isn't worth it!'

The truck thundered around the bend towards them. Four bright spotlights flared from its bull-bar, flooding the ute's cabin.

Gabe was blinded! He heard Piper give a shout, half-fright, half-frustration, and a heartbeat later he lunged sideways, grabbing the steering wheel and wrenching it hard to the left. The ute teetered dangerously, then plunged into the scrub at the side of the road.

There was a small tree in their path, but they ploughed straight ahead, sheering it off with their bull-bar.

Behind them, the cattle truck roared past.

In the rear-vision mirror he caught a brief, blurred glimpse of the shadowy but unmistakable shapes of cattle in the rear. Then, in front of them, the ute's engine seemed to die and a great spout of steam shot upwards into the black sky.

A burst radiator. Terrific.

He sank back, suddenly exhausted, his head pounding, his heart pounding harder. His stomach was lurching. He was shaking. Damn. His nerves were shot to pieces. He was a mess, slumped in the seat, eyes closed.

How could Piper have been so foolish?

Without opening his eyes, he forced himself to ask, 'Are you OK?'

He heard the thump of her hand as it punched the steering wheel. Heard her angry groan. 'How can I be OK? Those damn crooks got clear away with our cattle!'

Gabe felt ill and exhausted…world-weary… Her anger sounded so naïve. *Had he ever been like that?*

Yes, he had to admit—centuries ago—when he'd headed off for the army. He'd been desperate to prove his courage and daring. For many years the threat of danger had thrilled him rather than sobered him. It was only since his accident that he'd lost his appetite for unnecessary risk and danger. These days he felt completely separated from his old self, the man who'd wanted to take the world by the throat.

He opened his eyes and wondered if he had the energy to cope with Piper's bristling hostility.

'They wouldn't have ploughed into me,' she said. 'I would have forced them off the road. Why do women always have to be the ones to back down?'

'You didn't back down. I pulled the steering wheel out of your hands.' He sighed. 'It's only cattle, Piper.'

'*Only* cattle? They're *Windaroo* cattle. A sick old man's cattle—and they're worth hundreds of dollars each.'

'Piper, listen to yourself.' His strength returned as his anger mounted and he could hear emotion vibrating in his voice. 'No cattle, no amount of money, is worth risking your life!'

His words must have found their mark. He saw the stiffness leave her shoulders. Her mouth opened as if she was going to reply, but she changed her mind. She sat very still.

'Don't forget,' he added, 'I've been through a road smash. It's not a scene I want to revisit. I broke both my hands and my shoulder. And there are probably more metal parts in my right leg than in the front suspension of this ute. These days I'm more Bionic Man than Action Man.'

There was a sudden sparkling in her eyes, bright as the diamonds in her earlobes. Perfect. He'd made her cry.

Turning away, he scowled through the ute's side window. Outside, the slender trunks of eucalypt saplings gleamed in the faint moonlight like skinny, pale ghosts.

'Oh, Gabe,' he heard her whisper, and he felt the tentative touch of her hand on his cheek. Her fingertips trembled against his skin. 'I'm so sorry, Gabe,' she whispered. 'Please—'

His throat was choked and raw as he turned back. The silver sparkles in her eyes were spilling onto her cheeks. She withdrew her hand from his face and pressed those same shaking fingers hard against her lips, as if she were holding back a sob.

'I was being terribly selfish,' she said. 'How could I have forgotten what you've been through?'

He tried to swallow the pain in his throat. 'It's OK,' he said. 'Don't. Don't cry, Piper.'

He watched the way she hunched forward, her face sinking into her hands as the reality of their narrow escape took its toll, and the urge to reach for her was overwhelming. He wanted to pull her close. But he didn't trust himself. It would be madness to bring that soft, sweet mouth and tantalising body any closer. Madness to look too long into the soul-melting warmth of those lovely blue eyes.

He dropped his gaze to the dress, still draped across his lap, and that was no help either. It brought to life the image of her caught with her dusty denim jeans around her knees.

The white-as-moonlight curves of her breasts and bottom.

Oh, God! He'd drive himself crazy thinking about Piper that way!

His regret emerged as a deep sigh. 'I thought you understood that we didn't come out here to play heroes tonight.'

'I did, but then I got carried away. I was sick of following your orders like I was one of your underlings in the army.' Her teeth worried her lower lip. 'I don't know how I managed to forget about your accident, but I did. I'm sorry. It—it must have been horrendous for you.'

'Well...let's concentrate on what we need to do now.'

But Piper didn't seem ready to leave the matter alone. She fiddled nervously with one of her earrings as she asked, 'I suppose that's why you didn't ask me to dance, is it? Because of your bad leg?'

Oh, hell! Gabe cleared his throat as he searched for an answer. The stupid thing was, he didn't have one. When he'd walked into that ball tonight and seen Piper looking so damn amazing he'd been as flattened as the hypnotised youngsters around the bar. 'That's a silly question,' he said gruffly. 'Why would you want to dance with me when you were looking for a husband?'

Jerking her gaze away, her jaw jutted stubbornly. 'Yeah, well, it's just one bit of silliness after another for me tonight, isn't it?' They both stared awkwardly ahead into the black night. Finally she pointed through the windscreen to the escaping steam. 'What should we do now?'

'We'll need to call the Stock Squad. I'll take a walk and find a high spot in the mobile network.'

She considered his suggestion. 'There's a ridge straight through there,' she said, pointing into the dark to her right. 'I've got a torch in the glove box. I'll climb up there and ring Grandad and tell him what's happened so he won't sit up all night worrying about me.'

'Good thinking. Let's go.'

She depressed the door handle, then turned back to him. 'You stay here, Gabe. It might be a bit too steep for your leg. I know what to tell the Stock Squad.'

Gabe's jaw set stubbornly. Through gritted teeth he snarled, 'I can climb a little pimple of a hill.' And, before he completely lost his temper, he shoved the door open and leaped out of the ute.

## CHAPTER SIX

SHE was lying down.

Piper struggled to make sense of her surroundings. Above her she could see the ute's windscreen, and beyond that the black silhouette of gum trees against a scattering of stars. Her cheek was touching a cool swathe of silk. Her white dress.

*Holy smoke!* Beneath the thin fabric of her dress were firm thighs and the unmistakable bump of something masculine. Very masculine!

A jolt scorched through her! She was lying with her head in Gabe's lap!

And his hand was on her shoulder. His broad thumb lay just inside her collar, resting casually against her bare skin.

From where she lay she could see the shadowy underside of his strong jaw. The column of his throat emerging from the crisp white collar of his evening shirt. He'd removed his bow tie and loosened the collar and there was a hint of dark hair in the V of the shirt.

He must have sensed she was awake and looked down at her. And there was a tenderness in his gaze that stole her breath.

'You're awake, moondust.' His voice was incredibly gentle. And he didn't remove his hand.

She tried to speak but couldn't. Her tongue wouldn't work. How long had she been lying here with her head nestling on Gabe? How had it happened?

She struggled to remember. There'd been the long,

steep hike up the hill, the phone calls to Grandad and the police, the scramble back down through the scrub to the ute. She could remember that she and Gabe had been sitting in the ute talking about—what the heck *had* they been talking about? All she could remember was yawning.

'How long have I been asleep?' she asked.

'Oh, about an hour.' His thumb stroked her collarbone very slowly. Just once. And her skin tingled. Somehow she was quite sure he had done that while she was asleep.

'Don't worry,' Gabe said, smiling. 'You snore very politely.'

It was enough to shred the melting moment. Embarrassed, she shot out of his lap and into a sitting position behind the steering wheel, fighting back with a waspish challenge. 'Why on earth did you let me fall asleep?'

'You were tired. And I'm afraid I can be very boring company.'

'But—' She flapped her hands helplessly as she imagined the way he must have settled her head onto his lap and lifted her legs so that she was curled comfortably across the bench seat. 'What time is it?'

'Just after one.' He didn't seem the slightest bit flustered by the fact that she'd spent sixty minutes with her head in his lap.

'Any sign of the Stock Squad?' She forced herself to ask.

'Not yet.'

They lapsed into silence and Piper wished she was asleep again. Conversation with Gabe had never seemed so difficult.

'So what sort of fabric is this?'

He was rubbing her gown gently between fingers and

thumb. His hand looked incredibly dark and strong and male against the soft, slinky fabric.

'It's silk,' she said tightly.

'Thought it must be.' He dipped his head towards it. 'I can smell your perfume.' He sniffed. 'Nice. Very nice.'

She felt stupid for asking, but she couldn't help blurting out, 'So it passes the test?'

He frowned. 'What test?'

'The sense test. Remember you told me that a woman's perfume should be delicate—to complement her—ah—femininity?'

'Oh, yes,' he said. 'That test.'

'The stuff I bought ought to smell good; it cost eighty dollars.' She smiled. ' Grandpa reckons it smells better than bread in the oven.'

Gabe chuckled. 'Well, he's right. And it even smells better than Christmas dinner.' He lifted the dress close to his face. 'Actually, Piper, you got your money's worth. It smells very feminine. Fresh and flowery, like—'

He broke off as the rattle of an approaching motor sounded from down the track. Light danced in the ute's cabin. Piper wasn't sure whether she was pleased or not to see the Stock Squad truck bumping towards them along the rough bush road. As it pulled up she scrambled out of the ute and heard Gabe's door open.

Norm Harper leaned out of the window. 'Morning, folks.'

The knowing smirk in Norm's voice made her unnecessarily flustered and blushing. Her hands strayed to her hair. April's sophisticated upswept hairdo had suffered greatly from the evening's activities—not the least of which had been sleeping in Gabe's lap! Strands were falling down all over the place.

What would Norm make of her appearance? Her false eyelashes, pearl and diamond earrings and the tumbling remains of a glamorous hairstyle teamed with an old and torn work shirt and grubby, ripped jeans! And, just to complete the picture, cheeks as hot as two bush fires!

Grateful for the dark, she cleared her throat. 'Hi, Norm. It's—it's good of you to come out at this late hour.'

She saw Norm's eyes widen at her uncharacteristic formality. 'It's my job, isn't it?'

'Yes,' she said quickly. 'Actually, it's a pity you couldn't have been here with us earlier. Were you able to stop the cattle truck?'

'We stopped 'em all right,' Norm said. 'But the truck was clean.'

'Clean?' she cried shrilly. 'But I saw cattle. There were beasts in the back of that truck when they went past here.' Hands on hips, she turned back to Gabe. 'You saw cattle, didn't you?'

'I thought so,' he answered carefully. 'Just as we were forced off the road. I thought I caught a glimpse of quite a few cattle. But we were blinded by those spotlights, so I couldn't swear—'

Furious, Piper swivelled back to Norm. 'They definitely had cattle when they went past here.'

'They probably dumped the evidence,' Gabe suggested.

'If they thought you were suspicious they could have let the stock go again before I caught up with them,' Norm admitted.

'Did you get their names?' Gabe asked.

'Yep. It was Karl Findley and two of his stockmen. Do you know him? He has a property called Red Ridge.'

'I know the place,' Piper said. 'It's not very productive—on rough country, up the far end of the valley.' She scowled. 'He's probably been having a high old time swiping cattle that have been feeding on good pasture.'

'Well, he had an excuse all ready for me. Reckons he always uses this track as a shortcut.'

'Bulldust. A shortcut to a quick fortune.' Piper scanned the bush around them. 'As soon as it's light I'll be doing a muster right along this road and I bet I'll find a mob of cattle with Windaroo brands.'

'You're probably right.' Norm sighed. 'It's damn frustrating, but don't worry—we'll be keeping a close eye on those fellas from now on.' His voice held a smile as he added, 'Say, do you two want a lift back home? Or are you are you having too much fun out here on your own?'

The cheek of him! 'We're coming,' she growled.

As she hurried around to the passenger's door she hurled a hasty order over her shoulder to Gabe. 'Hurry up.'

But he didn't follow immediately. He went back to the ute for something. She heard the squeak of the ute's door opening and then banging shut, and when he finally squeezed into Norm's truck beside her he was carrying her white silk dress. His smile twinkled. 'Better not leave this behind.'

Piper cringed as she saw Norm's smirk widen. Good grief! Now he would suppose that Gabe had been filling in time by helping her out of her ballgown.

Her embarrassed glare swung from one man to the other and she felt her skin flame again. 'I—I had to get changed. I didn't want to gad about the bush in a gown—so I—'

Her stammering explanation didn't help matters at all.

Norm merely chuckled. 'Whatever you reckon, Piper.' He started up the truck. 'I'm getting home to bed.'

The sun was setting on another day before Piper and Gabe found the scattered mob of Windaroo cattle and got them all safely mustered back into the correct paddock. Piper was triumphant. 'Fifty head of cattle saved!'

The only thing that dampened her excitement was her grandfather's reaction.

'There's something bothering you, isn't there?' she asked him.

'Did you say the fellow in the truck's name was Karl Findley?'

'That's right. He runs Red Ridge station. He's not a mate of yours, is he?'

'No, but that real estate fellow who was out here last week mentioned his name. I think Findley's a potential buyer for this place.'

'Not any more!'

Michael didn't respond and Piper's eyes widened with horror. 'Good heavens, Grandad! You wouldn't dream of selling to a scoundrel like him!'

'I guess not.' Michael sighed. 'If only I wasn't so damn old and weak. These days I'm as useless as a wooden leg in a bush fire.'

The regret in his tired old face sent Piper hurrying to his side. Perching on the arm of his chair, she hugged him and kissed his cheek and tried not to think of how frail he felt. 'You silly old sweetheart,' she murmured 'You're the very best grandfather in the world.'

'Thanks, love,' he said. 'I've had a good life. Lots of

hard work, but lots of laughter, too.' He gave her arm a grateful squeeze. 'And lots of love.'

Piper rubbed her cheek against his soft silvery hair. 'I was remembering today how much fun we used to have—you, Roy, Gabe and me—when we used to all go mustering together. We had the best time.'

'Yeah.' He chuckled. 'But you were a scallywag, Piper. I was just thinking this morning about that time you put a dead snake in Gabe's swag.'

She smiled. 'He jumped back so fast he overbalanced into the creek.' She shrugged and pulled a face. 'I'm sure he deserved it.'

Michael tipped his head to one side and looked at her curiously.

'Well,' she said, feeling compelled to explain her comment, 'he'd probably been calling me horrible names.'

'The only names Gabe ever called you were cute nick-names, like wallaby or possum or—'

'Or chicken pox,' she supplied quickly. 'And if he really wanted to insult me, he'd call me a girl.'

*Or moondust...* a voice whispered. Last night he'd called her moondust, and it had sounded the very opposite of insulting...

Not that it meant anything. Not a thing!

This evening, when they'd come back from the muster, Gabe had been remote and withdrawn—almost surly—and he'd hurried off to Edenvale as if the hounds of hell were after him.

'I must remember that snake trick,' she mused, her mouth quirking into a grim little smile. 'I might need to put Gabe in his place some time.'

Her grandfather looked at her oddly again, and for a moment she thought he was going to comment. His mouth opened, but then he snapped it shut as if he'd changed his mind. 'You never told me much about last night's ball,' he said.

Oh, boy. Piper straightened. She'd hoped to avoid having to talk about the ball. 'It was fine. It was—great.' She forced a smile.

'You had plenty of dances?'

'I—I danced as much as I wanted to.'

'And Gabe turned up after all?'

'Yes.' She darted her eyes away from his questioning gaze. 'But then we found out about the cattle duffers...'

Michael shook his head. 'You shouldn't have had to leave the ball.'

'I didn't mind.' She jumped to her feet. Grandad seemed to work Gabe into every conversation and it always made her edgy and squirmy in the stomach.

'Last night was long and tiring and today's been hard work,' she said, yawning for extra effect. 'I'm thinking of having a quick meal and an early night.'

'Yes, you poor girl. You must be dead on your feet.'

'Beans on toast be OK for tea?'

'They'd be lovely, darlin'.'

Gabe was troubled.

Troubled enough to be prowling around Edenvale's billabong in the moonlight while his family sat in the lounge room watching after-dinner television. He was so restless that he'd almost borrowed a pack of cigarettes from Jonno. But he hadn't smoked in years and he didn't really want to start again now.

He kicked at a tuft of grass and sent gravel spraying onto the water. The sound disturbed a flock of black ducks and they took off with a whisper and a rush of wings, their departure rippling the billabong's surface, fracturing reflected moonlight into a thousand little rectangles.

Shoving his hands deep into the pockets of his jeans, he watched the scattering moonlight. At the far end of the billabong flying foxes were screeching and squabbling over blossom in the melaleucas.

As Gabe listened to them, he realised he was smiling. He hadn't expected to find so much pleasure in being back in the bush. On the muster with Piper today he'd ridden a horse for the first time in a year and despite his lack of sleep the previous night, the quiet serenity of the bush had given him a renewed sense of strength. Even the mute dignity of the cattle as they'd trotted obediently before him had seemed to be teaching him a lesson in acceptance.

Tonight, as he looked around him at the pale paddocks dotted with quietly moving cattle and the mobs of kangaroos moving soundlessly among the beasts, pausing to crop the tough grass before slowly loping off again, he recognised a deep, subterranean change in him.

It had been happening slowly, ever since the accident, but he was beginning to look at the outback with new eyes. The flat, extended plains and the familiar vegetation—the very things he'd rejected as an angry young man with an urge to travel and conquer the skies—seemed to restore his spirits now.

But a renewed fondness for the bush was a plus. It wasn't what troubled him.

What troubled him was Piper.

She was getting to him in ways he'd never expected. It was as if he was seeing her with new eyes, too. He found himself thinking about her every waking moment and half the time he was asleep, if his dreams were anything to go by.

Hell, he'd always had a deep affection for the kid, but he'd never thought of her before as a desirable woman. He hadn't even thought about whether or not she was pretty.

She was just Piper. A cute kid. She'd always had pleasant even features—a delicate chin, a straight, faintly freckled nose and light blue eyes. Her sweet and open face had always been expressive, making it hard for her to hide her feelings.

But last night she'd looked so adult. So impossibly beautiful, standing in brave defiance as she faced the line of stunned boys at the bar. And then, heaven help him, half dressed as she changed in the car park…and later, worst of all, asleep with her head in his lap.

He'd been shocked to realise that he wanted her. Wanted her with an awful, aching hunger that went beyond the attraction he'd felt for any other woman. And now it was becoming an insane kind of torture to be near her.

Trouble indeed.

There was no way he could satisfy this desire. Piper was almost certainly a virgin, not the kind of woman who'd indulge in a fling. Besides, she was looking for a husband.

And Gabe wasn't looking for a wife.

A man contemplating marriage had to be able to trust the future. Gabe couldn't. The day a speeding semi-trailer had run a red light, life had revealed itself to be a fickle game of chance. Since the accident he hadn't been able to look to the future with any sense of surety. One day at a time was about the best he could manage.

He reached the southern end of the billabong, stopped, took several deep breaths and let out a long, bleak sigh. Looking back to the Edenvale homestead, he saw that the lights were going out, one by one. His parents and Jonno were going to bed.

He should have made an effort to talk to them tonight. His family were probably as bewildered as he was by his moodiness of late. Tomorrow. He'd make a big effort to be extra sociable tomorrow.

'Gabe.'

As he reached the top of the steps the unexpected voice came out of the shadows on the verandah.

'Mum? What are you doing sitting in the dark?'

There was just enough creamy moonlight for him to see Eleanor Rivers at one end of a cane lounger.

'I've been waiting for you.' She smiled and patted the blue and white striped cushion beside her. 'Take a seat for a minute. I won't keep you long.'

'Is anything the matter?' he asked as he sat where she indicated.

'That's what I wanted to ask you, son.'

Gabe looked away. 'I'm fine.'

'But not as fine as you'd like to be. You've been down at the billabong. You've always gone there when you're really bothered about something.' When he didn't reply, she went on, 'I'm thrilled to see you looking so fit and strong again.'

'Yeah. I'm a walking miracle.' He regretted the bitterness in his answer as soon as it was out, but it was too late to take it back.

'Gabe,' she said gently, 'you may have forgotten that I used to be a nurse, but I remember some rather surprising things I learned about the way wounds heal.'

In spite of his reluctance to talk about this, Gabe was curious. 'Yeah?'

'There's always so much attention paid to the physical

wounds. And fair enough—they're horrendous and painful—and visible. However,' she added, leaning closer, 'the emotional wounds are often overlooked because they're invisible. But sometimes they can be even deeper than the physical injuries and take longer to heal.' She placed a hand gently on his. 'And they always leave a tough scar.'

Gabe couldn't find a way to respond. It would be foolish to try to deny that his emotions hadn't been affected by the crash. He could still remember the moment of horror in hospital when he'd realised that, while his damaged body was growing stronger, nothing felt as if it were healing inside.

If he'd been injured during a military campaign there would have been debriefings with army psychologists. Post Traumatic Stress counselling.

However, he'd never found anyone who really understood the way he felt about his accident. The silent rage when he'd been forced to give up a job he loved.

On his own, he'd been working his way past it, but as he sat there with his mother's hand clasping his he felt a ridiculous need to hear her telling him that everything would be all right in the morning.

'You have to remember to be patient with yourself, Gabe,' she said. 'It's going to take time before your future becomes clear.' Then she gave him the hug he needed.

He was blinking back tears when she released him.

'You have to believe that everything will make sense in time, son,' she said.

'I guess so.'

'I know it will.'

For several minutes they sat together, wrapped in a

warm cocoon of silence, then Eleanor asked suddenly, 'How's Michael Delaney?'

Her change of subject was unexpected, and Gabe found himself answering without hesitation. 'I'd say he's not travelling too well. Every day he seems to look more tired and fragile.'

'I'll go to visit him again tomorrow, and I'll take him a pineapple upside-down cake. He's always loved them and grumbles that Piper's never learned how to make them.'

He nodded. 'Good idea.'

'And what about Piper?' she asked. 'How's she coping?'

He opened his mouth to answer, then hesitated. His mother waited, her face as unemotional and calm as a painted Madonna's. 'Naturally, she's very upset,' he said at last.

'It'll be very hard for her.' She folded her arms across her chest and released a brief chuckle.

Gabe shot her a sharp glance. 'What's funny about that?'

'I was wishing I'd seen her at the ball last night. Jonno said she looked absolutely gorgeous. Took everyone by surprise.'

His Adam's apple scraped painfully up and down and he sat rock-still, with his elbows resting on his knees and his hands together, fingers steepled. Where the hell was this conversation heading?

'That's the first time Piper's been to a ball, isn't it?' Eleanor persisted.

'I wouldn't know,' he lied.

'It's about time she had a social life. She'll need lots of friends when Michael's gone.'

He offered a grunt in reply.

Eleanor leaned forward and sat in a pose that mirrored his, with her elbows resting on her knees. But while he felt as tense as a cornered scrub bull, she looked totally relaxed.

'I suggested to Jonno that someone should take Piper to the Wattle Park picnic races. They always have a ball during that weekend, and it would be a wonderful chance for her to meet a wider spread of young people.'

Hairs rose on the back of Gabe's neck. He glared at his mother. 'Is Jonno taking her?'

'I don't think so,' she said. 'He's too busy tearing himself apart over his on-again-off-again affair with Suzanne Heath.' She rose quickly and smiled down at him. 'But after last night I'm sure there will be plenty of offers to take Piper to the races.'

'She'll like that,' he agreed. 'She's looking for a husband.'

His mother's eyes were as wide as her smile. 'About time,' she said, and then yawned rather deliberately. 'Well, darling, it's been good to chat, but I'm afraid it's way past my bedtime. Your father will be wanting his breakfast at the crack of dawn.'

'Night.' Gabe frowned as he watched her go. How had Piper and the Wattle Park races crept into a conversation about his emotional health?

One minute his mother calmed him with her serene confidence that all would be well, next she had him in a fever again. He stood, stretched cramped limbs, and with a pensive frown crossed the verandah and entered the house.

It irked him that Eleanor's casual comment about Piper could get his guts churning like an angry ants' nest. Perhaps he was being overly suspicious, but he couldn't help feeling that she'd been giving him a not so subtle prod in Windaroo's direction.

The whole situation was getting way too complicated. It was time to simplify it once and for all.

And out of the blue the answer came to him. There was really only one solution.

Piper had to be married. That would solve all his problems. Once she was another man's property—once he knew she was settled on Windaroo with a husband—he could leave with a clear conscience. He could get on with sorting out his own life.

The best thing he could do was to help her find this husband.

The sooner the better.

## CHAPTER SEVEN

THE Wattle Park races! Piper felt such a sudden whiz of excitement she almost dropped the clothes pegs she'd been holding and threw her arms around Gabe.

Go to a ball with him? Bet your boots! Wear her beautiful dress again? Too right. Stay at the ball and dance? With him? All night? Of course she would! She would love to.

The only thing that checked her enthusiasm was the stiff way he was standing and his frown as he stared at her clothes line of blinding white washing. 'The picnic races will give you an excellent chance to meet young men from outside the Mullinjim district,' he said.

*What?*

He drew his gaze back from the washing and his smile was slow and careful. 'I'm sure we'll unearth plenty of useful marriage candidates at Wattle Park.'

Her happiness collapsed, draining so swiftly out of her that when she looked down she almost expected to see it seeping like water into the parched grass at her feet.

'Thanks for the invitation,' she said, keeping her eyes downcast, 'but I can't go.' She dropped the pegs into a bucket and bundled a billowing bedsheet into a cane washing basket. 'I couldn't leave Grandad for a whole weekend.'

Without letting her eyes meet his, she removed pegs from the next sheet, dragged in a deep breath of laundry-and-sunshine fresh linen and hoped Gabe couldn't see how his backhanded invitation had hurt her.

It was stupid to feel hurt, but there it was. She seemed to have very little control over her feelings these days. They kept soaring and diving without warning.

And now she was ducking behind her washing so he couldn't see her disappointment. How could he do this? How could he look at her the way he'd been looking lately—all kind of soulful and tender and sweet, as if he wanted to—so that she wanted to—

Since when had he become so damn eager to help her find someone else to marry?

When she'd first asked him for help he'd been brimming with reasons why he wouldn't be suitable. And now suddenly he was an expert husband-finder! She clutched at the clothes line as her legs threatened to give way.

Gabe didn't seem to notice that she was wilting with disappointment. 'Michael can spare you for a weekend, Piper,' he said. 'He has Roy for company, and my mother has offered to stay with him, too.'

She lowered the sheet and stared at him. 'Your mother? Has she really?'

Gabe nodded and reached to take a row of pillow slips from the line. 'She used to be a nurse before she was married. I know that was a long time ago, but if she came over Michael would be in good hands.'

Clutching the sheet to her chest, she stood transfixed by the thought that Gabe and his mother were conspiring to find her a husband. Last week she would have been delighted. Why wasn't she delighted? Wasn't this what she wanted?

She realised she was staring at Gabe, watching the way he took down the washing and the play of muscles in his shoulders and back beneath the thin blue cotton of his shirt—watching the rhythmical flow of his body as he reached and lowered. Reached and lowered. Watching his strong hands as they lifted the pegs and tossed them into the bucket. How could a man look so sexy doing such a feminine task?

The breadth of his shoulders, the slimness of his hips, the way his faded jeans rode low over those hips... everything added up to a very watchable situation.

He caught her eyes on him as he glanced at her over his shoulder and sent her a puzzled smile. 'What's the matter?'

'Nothing,' she muttered, and shoved the sheet she'd been clutching into the washing basket. Idiot! She gave a little shake to rid herself of the need to gawk at him. 'It—it's very kind of Eleanor to offer to sit with Grandad.'

'So you'll come?'

Oh, shoot! Had she just talked herself into a corner? 'I don't think I can. I've just moved the weaner calves into their own paddock. They're going to need monitoring over the next couple of weeks.'

'We'd only be away for a weekend, Piper. Leave extra protein and calf pellets in their trough and they'll be fine.'

'I suppose so.' She eyed him warily. 'Would you promise that you won't order any of those Wattle Park guys to dance with me?'

Gabe smiled. These days when he smiled like that it sent sharp, painful shivers all the way through her.

'I promise I'll be on my best behaviour,' he said. 'So I take it I can go ahead and make our bookings?'

The last sheet was still pegged on the line, and a gust of wind caught it and sent it flapping into her face. She made a business of gathering it in. 'I need to think about it,' she said. 'I'll have to check with Grandad first.'

* * *

Michael Delaney stood at the kitchen window and watched the two figures over at the clothes line. Then he turned back to Roy, who'd come in to share an afternoon cuppa with him. 'Things are looking good, mate,' he said with a gleeful wink.

'Yeah?' Roy peered through the window to see what Michael was so cheerful about.

'Piper and Gabe are making each other mighty miserable.'

Roy scratched his bald spot. 'And you reckon that's good?'

'Too right.' Michael beamed. He shuffled back to the kitchen table where he had a pot of tea and two mugs ready and waiting. 'This is how it goes. If only one of them was miserable we'd have a problem on our hands, but when they're both as miserable as bandicoots on a burnt ridge we're laughing.'

'I don't get it,' sighed Roy, staring at Michael with such a puzzled look he almost went cross-eyed.

Michael sat down and began to pour strong tea into Roy's mug. 'You ever been in love, mate?'

The old stockman spluttered and sat down quickly. 'Can't remember.' He accepted his mug of tea and added three spoonfuls of sugar. As he stirred, he cleared his throat. 'Actually, I was in love once. Long time ago.'

'You sneaky devil. All these years I've known you and you've never let on.'

'Well…it didn't go all that well. It's not something a bloke talks about.'

'But you can remember how it felt?'

Roy took a sip of tea as he searched for his answer. Then he placed the mug carefully back on the table and sent Michael a shy smile. 'I was bloody terrified most of the time.'

'That's what I mean!' Michael exclaimed. He clapped a hand to his head. 'I remember when I first met my Mary, rest her sweet soul. Oh, Lord! Didn't she give me a hard time! All that agony! The nerves. The *Will she? Won't she?* The feeling that you'd slit your own throat if you couldn't win her.'

Roy cocked his head towards the window. 'You reckon that's what's going on out there?'

'A version of it, mate.' Michael took a long draught of tea, then lowered his mug thoughtfully. 'But these two are going to find it harder than most because they know each other too well.'

Roy sighed. 'You're losing me again, Mick. That don't make sense.'

'Well, the way I see it is this. Gabe looks at Piper and all he sees is the kid next door. And Piper looks at Gabe and she sees this big brother figure she's known all her life.'

'Yeah,' said Roy. 'So what's your point?'

'The point is,' said Michael, poking the air with his teaspoon, 'they've been taking another look at each other lately and they can't work out what they're seeing. They don't even recognise what's really going on.'

'But you reckon they're actually in love?'

There was a noise at the door and Piper bustled into the room, a laden washing basket in her arms. Her face looked pale and pinched around the mouth, and her blue eyes scanned the two old men without really seeing them.

'Want a cup of tea, love?' Michael asked.

As if she hadn't heard, she crossed the room and headed down the hall.

'What about Gabe?' Michael called after her. 'Is he coming in for a cuppa?'

She spun around so quickly Michael might have thought she'd been zapped with a cattle prod.

'What did you say about Gabe?' she asked.

His eyes caught Roy's and their telltale gleam proclaimed loudly and clearly *I told you so*. 'Did Gabe want to join us for a cup of tea?' he asked her.

'I wouldn't know.' Her chin lifted as she added coldly, 'I didn't ask him and it's too late now. He's already gone.'

Roy's face was awash with concern as he watched her hurry down the hall as if she couldn't drop the subject fast enough. He leaned forward, clasping his mug with both his battered old hands. 'You really want that pair to get together, don't you?'

Michael smiled fondly. 'I do, mate. I want it more than anything in the world. I could die happy if I knew Gabe was going to take care of my little girl.'

'But what if you're barking up the wrong tree, you silly old goat? You see them sniping at each other and decide it's some kind of secret sign that they're in love, but maybe that's because it's what you want to see. Maybe they really have grown apart over the past ten years or so.'

'You're wrong,' Michael cried, his voice croaking with the effort. But as he sat there, tracing nervous patterns over the geometric squares of the red gingham tablecloth, Roy's words took root. He slumped lower in his chair. 'Lord, do you really think I've got the wrong end of the stick?'

Roy scratched the top of his shiny head again. 'I don't know, mate. Maybe I should shut my trap. I don't know the first thing about romance. Wasn't much chop at it myself.'

'I'm sure they're meant for each other,' Michael whispered, more or less to himself. He drained the last of his tea, replaced his mug exactly in the centre of a gingham square and shot Roy a shrewd glance. 'Anyhow, I've had a word with my solicitor and I've done something I hope will make them come to their senses. All I can do now is pray that it works.'

## CHAPTER EIGHT

GABE was *not* having a ball.

The crazy thing was he should have been happy. Really happy. Cloud nine stuff. Everything was going according to plan.

Piper had finally agreed to come with him to Wattle Park, which meant he could start in earnest to supervise her husband-hunt.

And now they were at the ball and she was doing her bit...looking beautiful in that white gown again, pretty earrings, and this time her hair was free and falling like ripe corn silk to her bare shoulders. And, because she was dead keen to avoid a repeat of her Mullinjim experience, she was putting on an extra brave face—she was smiling and confident and poised.

And she was reaping rewards.

Half the young blades in the district had danced with her, and for the past forty minutes she'd received the undivided attention of one dashing young grazier in particular. In fact, he seemed totally smitten by her charms.

His name was Charles Kilgour and by coincidence—the kind of coincidence that happens all the time in the bush—he was the brother of one of her old schoolfriends, so they had plenty to talk about. In fact, they were getting along like a bush fire.

And that should have been terrific.

Good old Charles had everything going for him. He was tall, athletic in a wiry sort of way, blond. He had shiny white teeth, no dirt under his fingernails, and he was appropriately aged at around two years older than Piper. She seemed to be enjoying herself, letting his hand explore her lovely white back while she danced in his arms and sent him dazzling smiles as if he was flaming Prince Charming.

Problem was…

Gabe didn't like him. And, after asking around this evening, he'd soon discovered that when it came to women Charles Kilgour loved 'em and left 'em. Any hint of a woman getting serious made him slippery as a greased pig.

Gabe had been there when Charles and Piper met earlier in the afternoon in the bar tent where all racegoers gathered after the main events finished. She'd been wearing a chic new outfit—a sleeveless sky-blue linen dress with white polka dots and a surprisingly low, scooped back. She'd added a sophisticated blue straw hat. And sunglasses.

Gabe had never seen her in sunglasses. Normally, if the sun was too bright, she just pulled her akubra lower over her eyes and squinted. Today she'd been transformed into a glamorous and mysterious stranger.

Not that he'd minded. He'd felt rather proud of her. In a fatherly kind of way, of course.

Everything had gone well at first. They'd mingled with a group of young people and they'd shared some general chit-chat—the usual combination of horse and cattle talk interspersed with attempts at witty banter.

It had been very pleasant. Gabe had been quite relaxed. Even when Charles Kilgour had made a beeline for Piper early in the piece, he'd been cool.

Things had deteriorated just before the group had dispersed to get ready for the ball, when Charles had taken Gabe aside.

'Piper's a bit of all right, isn't she?' he said, with a leery smile that smacked of nudge-nudge, wink-wink.

Gabe grunted his agreement.

'Thought I'd check the lie of the land with you,' Charles continued out of the side of his mouth. 'Piper tells me you're not really her partner. Just a friend of the family. Right?'

Gabe's immediate reaction was a violent urge to pick the smirking young pup up by the ears, take him behind the tent and toss him into the industrial bin along with the empty beer cans. But somehow he restrained the urge. 'What's it to you?'

'I just want to make sure the coast is clear.'

Gabe's fists clenched. 'Coast's clear for what?'

That was when Charles took a step back and looked at Gabe with scornful pity, as if he was one chop short of a barbecue. 'I don't like poaching on another chap's territory, but if Piper's free I plan to make a play for her.'

'A *play* for her?' Gabe ground his teeth so hard his jaw almost locked. 'I should warn you she's—she's very—ah—*young*.'

'Young?' Charles frowned. 'How young?'

'I'm not talking about her age,' Gabe said, and unwelcome beads of sweat gathered under his collar. 'She hasn't done much socialising. Hasn't been out with a lot of guys.'

That was a lightbulb moment for young Charles. His blond eyebrows rose halfway up his forehead. 'Virgin, eh?'

Gabe's fist was so keen to connect with the other man's face he had to shove both his hands into his pockets.

'That's interesting…' Charles mused. 'But, mate,

someone's got to do the deed at some stage…I'm sure I'm willing to rise to the challenge.'

It was right after that comment that Gabe dragged Piper away.

And back at the hotel they had a ding-dong row in the corridor outside their rooms.

'What do you mean, I can't dance with Charles?' she shouted. 'Are you crazy?'

'Keep your voice down, Piper. Just take it from me. He's not your type.'

'He's exactly my type,' she hissed. 'He's a cattleman. He's twenty-five. His sister Angela was a good friend. And besides, I like him! How can I possibly decide if a man's a suitable husband if I can't even dance with him?'

Gabe knew she was being logical. Her anger was justified and his own reaction was way over the top. Over the top or not, he couldn't help it. He couldn't let her go to her doom. 'If you can't see what's wrong with that guy, you need serious instruction in how to smell a rat.'

'How dare you?'

She stormed into her room and slammed the door.

And Gabe knew he'd made a tactical error. No doubt his overreaction had pushed her even more surely towards Charles Kilgour, and there was no way he could dissuade her without sounding like a neurotic nursemaid.

So now here she was. At the ball. Proving her point. Spending half the bloody night Superglued to Chazza Killjoy.

It was enough to drive a man to drink.

Downing his beer, Gabe cast one more disgusted glare in Piper's direction before going through to the bar for another coldie. Old friends greeted him and kept him talking. They were concerned about his accident, pleased to see him back on deck, itching to tell him about their families, wanting to hear his plans…

By the time he returned to the ballroom Piper and Charles had disappeared.

'This is better,' Charles said, taking Piper by the hand and leading her out of the brightly lit hall towards the shadowy creek bank. 'It's much cooler out here.'

Her heartbeats scampered and tripped as she walked beside him. She tried to calm down by taking deep breaths. It was good to be out of the ballroom. This was what she wanted. To be outside with Charles. Away from The Watchdog's moody glare.

How on earth did Gabe think she could relax and enjoy herself while he did his big brother act from the sidelines? There was no way she could get to know other young men while Gabe breathed down her neck. He was supposed to be helping her find a husband, not hindering her.

The way he'd tried to warn her off Charles was unforgivable. Charles was perfect husband material. He was polite, attentive, and paid her flattering compliments. Tall and handsome too—in his own way.

And he was taking her into the clump of she-oaks that lined the edge of the creek.

Her stomach fluttered. Excitement edged with panic. She knew that Charles intended to kiss her and, by heaven, she was looking forward to it. Damn Gabe. He had no right to try to stop her enjoying another man's attention.

If this went well, she could be in with a chance. She might be able to make Charles fall in love with her. And then Windaroo would be safe. Grandad wouldn't sell it if she had someone like Charles willing to march to the altar. She shoved aside thoughts of Charles as some kind of sacrificial lamb and concentrated instead on a picture of them both in the future, with one or two children. A boy and girl, of course. Both blonde.

They reached the shadows and she resolved to enjoy kissing Charles. This was going to be nice. Very nice. When he drew her close, she relaxed against him. It was a good start; he was a nice height. She could rest her head on his shoulder quite comfortably. That was a handy thing in a husband.

'Have I told you how lovely you are?' Charles asked as he held her close.

She smiled against his shoulder. Yes, he had. About half a dozen times.

'I always thought fellows over at Mullinjim were a bit slow. I can't believe they let you get away.' He walked his fingers up her spine. 'But I'm very glad you're here.'

For some ridiculous reason Piper felt impatient. She didn't want Charles to talk. Especially if he was only going to say the same things over and over. If he was going to kiss her she'd like to get on with it. She lifted her lips, hoping to signal her intention before he began to talk again.

Her ploy worked. She heard his surprised exclamation and then his arms tightened around her and she felt his mouth settle over hers.

It was quite a nice kiss. In fact it felt rather good to have a man's arms around her, to lean against his strength and feel the pressure of his lips against hers. She felt relief wash through her and realised she'd been worried that the experience wouldn't be pleasurable.

'You're rather good at this,' Charles murmured.

'Thank you.'

They kissed some more—open-mouthed—and Piper continued to enjoy herself. Kissing Charles was the nicest kind of calming experience. She almost spoilt everything by remembering Gabe and the way his simple touch had sent heat flaring all over and through her.

*Concentrate on Charles.* She couldn't spoil things by thinking about *Gabe* now. Charles was the man who'd been giving her compliments. Charles was the one who had danced with her, paying her attention while Gabe stalked and scowled in the corner. Charles was very acceptable. In time, she would be quite interested in further intimacy with him.

But not yet.

When his hand cupped her breast, she pulled away.

He gave a nervous little laugh. 'You're so sexy, a guy forgets—'

Piper frowned. 'Forgets? What did you forget?'

'Ah…' He grimaced momentarily, then took her hands in both of his. 'I was forgetting we'd only just met.' He kissed her forehead. 'Tonight has been special.'

Piper smiled. 'It's been special for me, too.'

'I want to get to know you better—to discover everything about the real Piper O'Malley. If only you lived closer.'

'At least we have tomorrow,' she said.

His chest puffed and he beamed at her. 'Yes—you must spend the whole day with me. and I'll book a top notch dinner for us in the evening.'

'That would be lovely,' she said.

'Good.' That settled, Charles seemed quite satisfied. He tucked her hand inside his elbow and as they walked back to the ballroom, he said, 'After tomorrow we'll sort out how to see more of each other. I don't think I'm going to be able to let you out of my sight for long.'

Piper's lips drew up at the corners and she smiled smugly. How about that? She'd never expected to make so much progress in one short evening.

Gabe was waiting just inside the doorway.

He fixed them both with a black scowl and her heart sank.

*Don't let him embarrass me. I'll never forgive him if he makes a scene. He mustn't bully Charles. I couldn't bear it.*

'Excuse me, Charles,' Gabe said in a cold, cutting voice, 'I need to speak with Piper.'

'What do you want?' she asked, matching her voice to his icy tones.

'If you'd just step outside for a moment?'

Her chin lifted. 'Can't you tell me here?'

She saw the flicker of impatience in his eyes. 'No,' he said. 'I can't.'

A sudden thought filled her with alarm. 'It's not Grandad, is it? You haven't had bad news?'

He didn't answer, simply took her by the elbow and began to propel her back through the doorway while he issued an order to Charles over his shoulder. 'This won't take long. You go ahead and get a drink, mate.'

'Is it Grandad?' Piper asked again as Gabe hurried her away from the ballroom, his grip on her elbow so vise-like she had little choice but to keep up.

'No, Piper. Michael's fine. My mother will ring immediately if there's a problem.'

'So what are you dragging me out here for?' She tried to tug her arm away from his grasp and almost overbalanced in her spindly high heels. 'You can't just abduct me when I'm having a perfectly lovely evening.'

He didn't answer until they were well away from the hall. In fact Gabe had almost reached the glade of she-oaks where Charles had kissed her before he spoke. 'I've been checking out your lover boy.'

'I've told you to mind your own business. He's not some kind of criminal.'

'No, but if his sister's really a friend of yours she will probably warn you off him. He doesn't have a very nice track record.'

'Don't be ridiculous,' she hissed. 'He's not a race-horse.'

'And don't you be precious, Piper. You know I'm talking about the way he treats women.'

'I don't want to hear it.' She didn't. The gall of Gabe, to try to ruin her evening! 'You've no right to go around digging up dirt on my—my friend.'

'Friend? Huh! You've known him five minutes.'

'I don't care. And I don't give a hoot for anything you think you've found out. It's probably a lie, and any-how, there have been plenty of rumours about *you* in the past.'

Gabe's face tightened. 'That may be,' he said stiffly. 'But I'm not one of your suitors.'

She felt the sting of his words as if he'd slapped her. She *had* to sting back. 'Believe me, Gabe, I'm thanking my lucky stars you're not!' She glared at him through tear-blurred eyes. 'And I don't appreciate your snooping around. I've been quite—I've been very impressed by the way Charles has—ah—treated me.'

To her horrified surprise, Gabe shoved her roughly, deeper into the whispering trees. 'So you've had your first necking session with Romeo?'

Her hand flew to her lips. 'Don't be crude. I won't let you spoil this for me.'

He stood there, breathing harshly. 'Was it good,

Piper?' The question came in a breathless, rough whisper. 'Was it really special for you?'

One half of her brain told her she shouldn't be having this conversation. It was crazy. But another part of her wanted to hurt him. How had she ever been so naïve as to think of Gabe Rivers as her personal hero?

She lifted her chin and did her best to look down her nose at him. 'Since you insist on asking, I'll tell you. Yes, it was special, Gabe. It was wonderful. Kissing Charles was—was fantastic.'

'Bully for Charles.'

'He makes me forget I was ever a tomboy. He makes me feel very—*feminine*.'

For the shortest time Gabe's mouth fell slack, then he jerked his gaze away from her. Piper's heart gave a painful lurch, then seemed to stop beating all together.

When he looked back at her once more the she-oaks seemed to close in around them. She saw his lips curl slowly into a contemptuous smile. 'Hell, Piper, don't get fooled by the first bloke you try. Any man who kisses you will make you feel feminine. I bet if I kissed you the same thing would happen.'

*No!*

She tried to shout the word, but was paralysed by the immediate tension and heat that eddied and pooled low inside her. 'No,' she whispered, but it was so soft she was sure he didn't hear.

Calmly, mercilessly, he moved towards her. 'It's true, Piper,' he murmured. 'Any old kiss can make you feel like a woman.' Then he reached for her.

She tried to resist, but her bones seemed to have turned to syrup. She made one ineffectual flutter with her hands, as if to ward him off, but Gabe ignored it. He drew her against him and, with something like a growl, covered her mouth with his.

# CHAPTER NINE

NOTHING, absolutely nothing, could have prepared her.

There was no tenderness, no tentative caress. Without any prelude, his strong arms imprisoned her and his hostile mouth claimed hers. For a several frantic seconds she made attempts to resist, refusing to surrender to the demanding force of his lips.

Foolish thought. This was Gabe. And, whether she liked it or not, her heart was making decisions while her body melted and her mind turned to mush.

These big shoulders beneath her hands, this fierce body locked hard against hers, this warm, impassioned mouth moving over hers—all of it was Gabe.

As her nostrils filled with the scent of him any thought of resistance evaporated. All she could do was close her eyes and give herself up to sensation after delectable sensation. The special smell of his skin, spicy and clean like the wind in the trees. The possessive, urgent pressure of his body. The unyielding command of his lips.

Suddenly she knew she'd been waiting a lifetime for this moment. She couldn't waste it; she needed it. She had no choice but to link her hands behind his nape and kiss him back. And she felt a happy surge of surprise as Gabe's initial fierceness gave way to a slower but much more intimate exchange.

*Oh, yes…* His hands lingered to caress her bare back, and they were possessive hands, expert hands that boldly yet tenderly tested the texture of her skin and traced the shape of her hips and bottom through her silk gown.

*Yes...* Gabe's lips softened and grew more gently seductive. They moved over hers slowly, savouring her...as if he wanted to store memories of the taste and the feel of her. His tongue touched hers and her entire body quivered with a blissful, wild longing. *Yes! Yes!* She opened her lips and welcomed him into her.

Oh, the beautiful intimacy!

Their tongues met, learning and loving the shape and the taste of each other. Gabe lifted away for the briefest moment and then took her again. And again. Each time his mouth returned to reclaim her her happiness mounted.

*Oh, Gabe! Yes! Yes! Yes!*

She could feel her body becoming both heavy and languid, and yet tense with a strange impatience. Heat was swimming through her veins, reaching her breasts and her loins... How amazing to feel so much needy desire so soon. Heat and longing building up...urging her to surrender everything to this man.

Whatever, however Gabe demanded, she would be his.

Now.

For ever.

Whenever.

He lifted his lips from hers again. And this time she sensed him pull further away. *No!* She tilted her face closer, but he recoiled sharply, and instead of his heated mouth all she could feel was a cool breeze blowing over her wet lips.

Panic knifed through her. *No. He couldn't. He couldn't stop. Not now.*

'Gabe?' she cried in a choking voice.

For a moment she thought he was going to pull her back to him again. But, Lord help her, he was stepping further away, loosening his hold so abruptly she almost collapsed.

She swayed sideways and his hand shot out to steady her. *Kiss me again. Please, Gabe. Surely we can't let this magic stop?* The harshness of his breathing and the tremor in his hand told her that he was as shaken by their kiss as she was. But, apart from his hand at her elbow, he held the rest of his body carefully away from her.

'What's the matter?' she whispered, lifting a hand to touch his cheek.

'Don't,' he said abruptly, and he closed his eyes and jerked his head aside as if he couldn't bear to see the unmistakable emotion in her face. He kept his eyes tightly closed as he said, 'You've always been a handful, Piper. I should have listened to my better judgement. I hope you've learned your lesson now.'

*Lesson?*

*I hope you've learned your lesson.*

The words fell on her like stones. Pelting her.

Horrified, she stared at him. 'What are you saying?'

His eyes shot open again. Green-black, smouldering, tormented, lancing her with their ferocity. 'Did that kiss make you feel...*feminine*?'

No! He couldn't! He couldn't share with her the most beautifully intimate kiss since the beginning of time and then pretend it had been a mere lesson.

Tears choked her. She couldn't breathe. With one hand clutched to her painful throat, she struggled to control her panic. 'You're not going to pretend that this—this—this whole *incident* was nothing more than one of your stupid lessons?'

Once again he jerked his gaze from hers, and she saw his profile silhouetted against the light from the ballroom. The arrogant tilt of his head. The forward thrust of his jaw. Belligerence personified.

'That's exactly what it was.'

If she'd been braver she would have tossed her pride to the winds and told him that his experiment had failed, that he was completely, totally wrong. That his kiss had made her feel a thousand times more feminine than Charles's, that he'd made her experience with Charles—her pleasant experience with Charles—seem as sexy as flossing teeth.

But she couldn't challenge him with that.

The pride and the dark severity in his face rattled the bones of her courage and she had to settle for half the truth. 'I don't believe you,' she said.

Yet even those simple words found their mark. Gabe stiffened and drew his shoulders back, like a soldier standing to attention. Sphinx-still. It seemed an age before he slowly turned his head her way. 'You'd better believe me, Piper. It's the awful truth.'

She drooped as all the breath rushed out of her. What a silly little fool she'd been. All these years she'd imagined that Gabe was special.

He was a rat.

Only a monster could kiss her like that as a lesson!

She would have burst into tears if she hadn't been made of sterner stuff. Piper O'Malley had never been afraid of rats or monsters. She'd never been a scaredy-cat, wimpy girl. She'd spent too long being a tomboy. Being tough.

If she fell off her horse she got straight back on.

Straightening her shoulders, just as Gabe had straightened his, she fixed him with a bitter glare. 'Do you make a habit of teaching women lessons?'

'Only those who ask for them.' He shoved his hands

in his pockets and let out an exaggerated sigh. 'And then it's usually done with great reluctance.'

A disbelieving snort escaped her. 'Reluctance? Oh, yes, I noticed your *great* reluctance.'

'Get off your high horse, Piper. This wasn't my idea in the first place. Just cast your mind back to when we were in the scrub watching for cattle duffers and you pleaded for my help.'

The last thing she needed now was to be reminded of that night when she'd more or less begged him to kiss her. And he'd refused.

'You know what I'm like,' Gabe went on. 'If someone gives me a job I see it through. I feel responsible. But the first time I tell you you're going in the wrong direction, with the wrong bloke, you dismiss me out of hand and think you know it all.'

She sniffed disdainfully and tried to force a cold, dismissive smile. It felt more like a rather weak, disappointed little smile. 'You warned me about Charles, but who warned me about you?'

He blinked and looked bewildered.

'Charles didn't try to take advantage of me the way you just did,' she challenged, hastily shoving aside unwanted memories of her own response. 'Who's going to police the policeman?' When he didn't answer, she hurried on, 'Thanks for all the lessons, Gabe. You're right. You've taught me something very valuable tonight.'

'Glad to hear it.' His head tilted, as if he was waiting for her explanation.

'I understand now that I don't *need* or *want* your help. Not ever.'

His continued bewilderment strengthened her smile, and with regal dignity she turned and began to walk away from him. He moved as if to follow her. 'Stay there, Gabriel,' she snapped in a tone she might use with a cattle dog. 'Don't you dare follow me back into the ballroom. In fact I'd very much appreciate it if I don't have to clap eyes on your face for the rest of the weekend.'

It was very quiet outside as he watched Piper hurry into the hall. He saw the gleam of her golden hair and the delicacy of her slender form in its silky white gown as she paused in the brightly lit doorway, then disappeared into the hall to be lost amidst the noise and the laughter and music.

Gabe kicked at a stone, shoved his hands in his pockets and turned away, sick to the stomach over what he'd just done. What was he? Man or beast? He'd known as soon as his lips touched Piper's that he was making the biggest mistake of his life. He'd been wanting to kiss her for weeks and he'd given in to a moment of weakness.

But Piper had come alive in his arms in a way he could never have predicted. Little Piper! So passionate! Hell! He couldn't remember any woman who'd excited him more.

Without experience or art, she'd thrown herself into that kiss with the big-hearted enthusiasm she brought to every aspect of her life. She was such an intoxicating package. Why hadn't he been wiser? Surely he should have known she would taste so sweet. And in all honesty he couldn't pretend to be surprised that she'd felt so exquisitely soft and feminine and damn sexy.

But he could never have guessed that she would respond so sensually!

He'd been on the very edge of losing control.

Who was he trying to kid? He'd lost total control and then, angry with himself, he'd crushed her with his cruel claim that it had all been intentional. Part of his lesson! Huh! And he was supposed to be the expert!

Piper would be better off if he left her to Charles and made sure they headed safely up the aisle. So what if Charles was a bit of a womaniser? Piper was enough to settle any man down.

His mistake had been to get mixed up in this mess in the first place. Life had been simple and straightforward for twenty-three years. He and Piper had a no-nonsense big-brother-little-sister-style friendship. This husband-hunt of hers had ruined everything.

And he was left to pace the lonely creek bank with a churning stomach and a haunting guilty conscience.

Inside the hall, Piper found Charles looking tall and dapper but frowning petulantly as he waited for her. She paused for a moment and took a deep breath, before rushing over to him and offering her widest, most appreciative smile. 'I'm terribly sorry to have kept you waiting.'

He looked relieved and quite pleased. 'Is everything all right?'

'Absolutely fine,' she assured him.

'What did Rivers want?'

She lifted her right eyebrow into a fine arc and sent him a deliberately coy smile. 'He wanted to warn me off you.'

Charles grew red.

'Don't worry,' she murmured, patting his arm. 'I've no intention of listening to anything he says about any man I'm interested in.'

Charles brightened. 'Jealous, is he?'

'No, not at all,' she said quickly, hoping the sudden flare of heat in her cheeks didn't show. Heaven knew, she'd already asked herself that same question, hoping desperately to find a grain of evidence that it might be true. But, despite the convincing fervour he'd poured into his kiss, she couldn't believe that Gabe was jealous.

If he'd wanted her for himself he'd had ample opportunity to win her, but he'd never tried. 'He's been like that all my life,' she said. 'A constant pain in my butt.'

She smiled at Charles again, and silently reminded herself that she was grateful to Gabe for his painful but timely lesson. Without his rude interference she might never have appreciated how exceptionally *nice* it was to be with a man who didn't make her heart twist or her stomach tie itself in knots—who didn't hurt her cruelly—who didn't, in fact, disturb her in any way at all.

'This Chardonnay is the best in the house. It'll go very nicely with the chicken breast you've ordered.' Charles lifted his wine glass and squinted at it in the subdued lighting of the restaurant that was part of the Wattle Park Hotel.

Finnigans, Charles had told Piper, provided the finest dining in town. But she knew that wasn't saying a lot. The only competition was a café in the main street and a hamburger joint out along the highway.

This Sunday night it was so crowded with racegoers that they had been lucky to get a table for two midway down one side of the large square room.

The atmosphere was appropriately romantic—mood lighting, pristine table linen, gleaming silver, sparkling glassware, flowers and candles on every table, deep pile carpet and dramatic velvet wallpaper.

Piper drew in a breath and let it out with a relieved sigh. The perfect setting for her first real date!

Thank heavens she'd had the foresight to ring April

last week for more advice about clothes. Without a gentle shove from her elegant mentor she would never have lashed out and bought four new outfits, and she certainly wouldn't have been game to wear this little black dress. But tonight she felt confident that it was right. On the short side, a bit revealing, but exactly right.

So here she was on the perfect date, about to have a sophisticated conversation about wine. Only one small problem…two problems. She was ready to drop with weariness after the hectic weekend and she knew next to nothing about wine.

When she confessed her limited knowledge to Charles, he smiled indulgently.

'Would you like a lesson on how to appreciate these clever little grapes?'

To her embarrassment, a yawn escaped. 'Sorry, it's been a big weekend. All those racehorses' names to remember and so many people to bet on—I mean meet.' She flashed a smile. 'Of course I'd love to learn about wine.'

But her smile faltered. Holy heck! Could she handle another man teaching her another lesson tonight? She was still reeling from last night's.

She had to focus on why she was here with Charles. Had to remember her mission was to make him fall in love with her. OK, it was time for flattery. She pinned her smile back into place. 'It's nice to meet a cattleman who's not a country hick. I think it's terribly important for a man to be sophisticated, no matter where he lives.'

Charles grew pink with delight.

'So what do I do?' she asked. 'Am I supposed to sniff the wine first?'

He picked his glass up by the stem and she noticed

how slender his hand was. Funny, she hadn't seen that before. 'You should swill it gently...'

She swilled.

'Gently, Piper. Don't slosh it over the rim.'

'Sorry.' She steadied her movements. 'Why are we doing this?'

'To release volatile vapours and strengthen the scent.'

'I see.'

'Watch this,' said Charles, and Piper watched as he made a performance of sticking his nose deep into his glass. Apparently satisfied with that experience, he took a decent sip of wine, held the liquid in his mouth for a few moments, then raised his eyes to the ceiling and wiggled his lips around before swallowing.

She scolded herself for unkind thoughts about how he looked. 'What's the verdict?'

'Ah!' he sighed, then nodded thoughtfully and pronounced with a lofty smile, 'It's a superb drop. Pale, crisp, restrained, focused, but not—'

'Oh, no!' Her groan was completely inappropriate, but just at that moment her attention was caught by a tall, dark figure striding into the restaurant.

'What's the matter?' Charles looked puzzled as she stared at a point behind him.

'My bodyguard has turned up.' She glared at Gabe, who was being shown to a table just two places behind Charles.

Peering over his shoulder, Charles sighed. 'I don't get this. Gabriel Rivers has been trailing you like a bad smell all weekend, but I thought I'd gained clearance.'

Piper frowned. 'Clearance?'

With a self-conscious pursing of his mouth, Charles leaned forward and took her hand. 'As soon as I saw you I knew I wanted to...to get to know you very well, so I checked with Gabe to make sure you weren't his girl.'

'Oh.' Piper grabbed her wine glass with the hand Charles wasn't holding and swallowed a huge, unlady-like, undignified gulp of Chardonnay.

Behind Charles's back, she could see the waiter bringing Gabe a glass of dark red wine. As soon as the waiter left Gabe lifted it and with an annoying grin and a dip of his head made a saluting gesture towards her.

She whipped her eyes back to Charles and favoured him with a dazzling smile.

Charles said, 'Gabe Rivers is the last guy I want to tangle with.'

'Oh, pooh,' she scoffed. 'You don't have to worry about him. He's harmless.'

'Oh, yeah, sure. Very harmless.' Charles rolled his eyes. 'He looks at death's door, doesn't he? Don't kid yourself, Piper. Gabe Rivers might have suffered a few injuries, but I'm willing to bet he's still the toughest man in the district.'

She hid her surprise by lifting her wine glass again. 'Let's not spoil a delightful evening by talking about a despicable toad.'

When Charles frowned, Piper wondered if she'd overdone the criticism. He might suspect she was protesting too much. 'What else were you going to tell me about wine appreciation?' she asked, forcing her eyes wide in an effort to look immensely interested.

'Well,' said Charles, puffing his chest importantly, 'it's a matter of educating your senses...'

She tried.

She honestly tried to ignore Gabe while she listened to Charlie's wine-tasting lecture. The problem was Gabe was right there, in her line of sight. And Charles was talking about her sense of smell and taste, and she was remembering another night and another discussion with that other man…about the senses of smell and taste and *touch*…

She tried to move her chair so that Charles blocked her view of Gabe, but somehow next time she looked up he was there again.

Their eyes kept meeting, and each time Piper looked away quickly. But Gabe's green-eyed gaze seemed to taunt her and it was so hard to avoid thinking about last night's kiss. Good grief! She'd been an absolute wild creature in his arms. She couldn't believe she'd felt so passionate. Just thinking about it again set her nerves jangling with embarrassment—and, heaven help her, with longing!

Damn Gabe. Yes, double damn him! She slammed her wine glass down so hard she slopped more wine out onto the starched linen tablecloth.

'Sorry,' she told Charles meekly.

'You seem very on edge.'

'I know. I'm sorry. I think I must be more tired than I realised. It's been a huge weekend.'

Charles raised the hand he'd been holding and his eyes glowed with genuine warmth as he touched his lips to her fingers. 'It's been a truly wonderful weekend,' he said. 'I for one will never forget it.'

'Oh, Charles,' she murmured, wishing she felt more in tune with this very romantic moment, knowing she would be much more in tune if a certain moron wasn't grinning at her from over Charles's shoulder!

What a show pony! Gabe ground his teeth as he watched the other man holding his wine up to the light, swilling and sniffing and smirking.

Too much more of this and he knew he would do something that would seriously provoke Piper. Her eyes had flashed her annoyance the moment he arrived.

After his own bad form last night he was prepared to give Charles Kilgour a chance, but she deserved so much better. He couldn't sit here and let that painful poser worm his weasely way into her affections.

When she shot a drop-dead glare his way, Gabe scowled back at her. He'd always thought she had a healthy dose of common sense and a generous dollop of good taste, but she really looked as if she was falling for the dubious charms of this performing seal.

No doubt Charles was planning to ply her with fine food and wine so that straight after dinner he could charm her right out of her little black dress—her *very little* black dress.

Gabe took a sip of his wine and tried to relax. But the situation was getting desperate. Charles was kissing Piper's hand again. And she was looking at him as if he was the cat's meow.

He cursed under his breath. Michael would never forgive him if he left Piper to the mercy of this cardboard cut-out of a real man. The way things were heading, old Kilgour might not wait till the end of the meal to take her back to his room.

That thought was enough to make a man do something rash.

# CHAPTER TEN

PIPER tried not to look at Gabe, but there he was again, right in her line of sight over Charles's shoulder. She dropped her gaze to the tablecloth. This was a proper date. Her first proper date with a man and she was making excellent progress. She couldn't let Gabe spoil this!

She wanted Windaroo so badly! And Charles's kiss last night had been nice enough…

Charles kissed her hand again and—and *damn Gabe! What game was he playing at now?* Her jaw dropped as she watched him roll up his napkin and hold it to his eye like a spyglass! The man was a pirate! He was trying to sabotage her date.

Luckily, Charles was busy playing with her fingers and didn't notice how distracted she was. With her free hand she sent frantic signals for Gabe to stop and pointed to the door.

'God, you're gorgeous,' Charles said, and to Piper's surprise, he leaned right across the table and planted a kiss smack on her lips.

Such a public display of affection startled her, and she didn't exactly enjoy the kiss, but she enjoyed Gabe's response much less. Out of the corner of her eye she saw him raising his hand to wave at her. Heavens, he was grinning broadly and giving her the thumbs-up signal as if to congratulate her!

*Enough!*

She didn't have to put up with this!

'Excuse me,' she muttered, slipping her hand from Charles's grasp and jumping to her feet.

There was only so much a girl could take, and Gabe Rivers had overstepped the mark. Like a heat-seeking missile, she zeroed straight in on his table.

Anger bristled from every pore. She'd never been so mad! Heaven help her! For the past twenty-four hours she'd been angry because Gabe had kissed her. Angry because he'd stopped kissing her. Angry because he'd aroused her and made her feel things she'd never wanted to feel. Angry because he didn't want her and had so easily handed her back to Charles.

But angriest of all because he was *here*. Now. Spoiling her chances of a secure future.

She was fit to burst. 'What do you think you're doing?'

One of his dark, elegant eyebrows lifted as he regarded her with amused astonishment. 'I'm dining.'

Her breath came in short, shallow gasps and she clutched the back of the empty chair opposite him.

'A man has to eat,' he said.

'But you don't have to eat here.'

'I do if I care about my digestion. I didn't fancy a greasy hamburger.'

'I mean here. At *this* table.' Her hand came down on the tabletop with a thump. 'In that chair where you can stare at us—at *me*!'

He looked around at the crowded restaurant with an air of helpless innocence. 'This is where the waiter placed me. Besides,' he added with a slow, annoying smile, 'whether you like it or not, I'm still on the job.'

'What job?'

'Supervising your husband-hunt.'

Hands on hips, she looked down at him with a bitter

sneer. 'I told you last night, you're sacked. Anyhow, I would have thought someone who'd worked with the SAS would be able to conduct surveillance in a slightly less obvious manner. Move, Gabe. Now.'

He cast another slow glance over the nearby tables of diners. 'You're not worried that people will think your request a little odd?'

'Not in the least.' She wished her breathing was calmer. 'You can have your meal sent to your room. Now, are you going to move?'

'I'd prefer to stay here. What's the problem, Piper? You seem to be making great progress over there with Charlie. You two are very pally. But he might get his sensitive nose out of joint if you spend half the night here, talking to me.'

She leaned lower and hissed through gritted teeth. 'You know you're spoiling my night and you're making a ridiculous exhibition of yourself!'

'*I'm* making a show of myself?' He laughed silkily. 'Your bloke's the one putting on the show—sticking his schnozz halfway down a wine glass.'

Her reaction was as inevitable as the lightning that comes with thunder. Her hand snaked forward and she snatched up his glass of red wine and tipped it over his head.

The claret travelled quickly. It ran in little blood-coloured rivers through his hair, down his face, pooling in the valley where his starched white collar sat against his neck. Some of it continued on down, making a bright, bloody stain on his snowy shirtfront.

Piper gasped at her audacity. And all around her she could hear echoing gasps from stunned diners. Then frozen, astonished silence.

Not one clink of cutlery or glassware.

Gabe's face was a grim mask. He sat very still and stared straight ahead, not linking eyes with anyone. Piper sensed movement behind her, and shot a quick glance back to see Charles rising to his feet.

She felt numbed with the shock of her own actions. The wine was so dark against the white of Gabe's shirt. His face was so stony. The restaurant was so full. This was so embarrassing. How could she have been so stupid?

A waiter appeared at Gabe's side. 'There's a phone call for you, Mr Rivers,' he said, and then he saw the dark liquid dribbling down Gabe's neck, the mulberry-coloured stain. 'Oh, goodness, sir.'

Unwilling to meet the waiter's gaze, Piper shot another frantic glance in Charles's direction. His pale eyes seemed to be popping out of their sockets and his ruddy face reflected extreme mortification. She took a hesitant step towards him, but he shook his head at her and raised one hand as if to ward her off. He looked for all the world as if he was deterring a pack of vampires with his trusty crucifix. Then, turning abruptly, he scurried across the restaurant towards a rear exit.

'Oh, dear, oh, dear,' she heard Gabe drawl. 'Don't tell me you've shocked poor Charles.'

'Mr Rivers?' the waiter said again. 'About the phone call…'

'Ah, yes.' Ignoring the trickling wine, Gabe switched his full attention to the waiter. 'Who's calling?'

'Mrs Eleanor Rivers. She's concerned about a Mr Delaney.'

*Grandad!*

Piper's heart felt as if it had been struck by an enormous gong.

Gabe leapt to his feet. 'Where's the phone?'

'If you'll follow me, sir.'

Together they hurried towards the reception desk. Gabe made no attempt to wipe away the wine on his face and Piper stumbled behind him, no longer caring that every head in the restaurant was turned their way. All she could see was Grandad. His darling old face creased with laughter lines…

*Please, God. Don't let him be dead. Please, please… not yet. Don't take him yet.*

They reached the counter, and as Gabe grabbed the phone she stood beside him, stiff with fear, one hand holding her stomach and the other pressed against her mouth.

'Gabe, here,' he said. 'How are things, Mum?'

Piper could hear Eleanor's voice on the other end of the line but she couldn't make out her words. Her heart pounded as she watched the concentration on Gabe's face. He listened carefully, nodding without speaking. Just once his worried glance linked with hers and a sharp stab of fear shot through her, but he looked away again.

Finally he said, 'OK. Thanks, Mum. We'll come straight away.'

*No!*

He put down the phone and turned to her, his voice gentle as he said, 'Michael's had another heart attack.'

She had to cover her open mouth with both hands to hold back the urge to cry out.

'He's in the ambulance now. On his way to Mullinjim Hospital.'

She nodded, hot tears coursing down her cheeks. The poor darling. He needed her.

With a supportive hand at her elbow, Gabe said, 'I'll take you there straight away.'

She whispered her thanks as he turned quickly to the

receptionist behind the desk. 'Send me the bill for Miss O'Malley and myself. We'll be leaving immediately.'

The woman's questioning eyes had been taking in the embarrassing claret stains on his skin and clothing, but his instructions were given with such an air of authority that she didn't bat an eyelid as she replied, 'Of course, sir.'

As Gabe's car shot down the highway towards Mullinjim Piper sat huddled in the passenger's seat, her mind a horrified daze. 'Did your mother say how bad Grandad was?'

'Not exactly, but she sounded rather worried.' His hand thumped the steering wheel. 'I wish I had a chopper with me. I could get you there so much faster.'

Even if they broke speed limits the journey would take close to three hours. Three agonising hours! What might happen to Grandad in all that time?

In the headlights of an oncoming car she saw the frustrated clench of his jaw. 'I don't suppose you enjoy driving cars any more—since the accident.'

'I'm not nervous about driving on the road. But cars are so damn slow.'

They lapsed into silence while Gabe concentrated on his driving. At least he'd dropped the silly behaviour that had been annoying her all weekend. All it had taken was the news about Michael and he'd been transformed back into her good old dependable friend again.

Beyond the car a crescent moon rode high in the heavens, dipping and bobbing through wisps of cloud like a ship at sea.

Piper kept seeing visions of Michael, lying still and white in a hospital bed, with horrid tubes and machines plugged into him and medical staff buzzing around him.

Her mind winged back through memories of her childhood—Grandad teaching her to ride, showing her how to make formula for the calves, nursing her through chicken pox, meeting her at the railway station every time she came home from boarding school, putting up with her teenage tantrums…telling her always how much he loved her, how proud he was.

She knew she'd been a handful, but Michael had always been so patient with her.

'I was only a year old when Grandad was lumped with having to raise me,' she said.

Gabe flashed her a quick smile. 'Michael was crazy about you from the day you were born. I remember the day he came tearing over to our place to tell us the news of Bella's baby girl. He was so excited he gave me a cigar, even though I was only six years old.'

Piper managed to smile through a sheen of tears. 'Did you smoke it?'

'Two puffs and I was sick as a dog. Put me off cigars for life.'

They exchanged brief grins.

'Tell me he's going to be all right,' she whispered.

For the longest time Gabe didn't answer, but then he said gently, 'Whatever happens, he'll be all right, Piper.'

It wasn't quite the answer she wanted to hear, but she knew in her heart it was true. But then she thought of the little churchyard in Mullinjim, with its row of golden wattle trees shielding it from the road and the headstones in one corner—for Mary Delaney, her grandmother, and for Peter and Bella O'Malley, her parents.

The thought of the terrible and lonely battle Michael Delaney was fighting and the possibility that he might soon join the others sent twin rivers of silent tears streaming down her cheeks.

As the slow miles inched by she grew cold, and rubbed her arms to try to warm them. Her little black dress with its tiny straps and short skirt was rather inadequate now, but at least her legs were covered by black nylon stockings. Oh, Lord! Looking at those filmy stockings reminded her of the restaurant and her astonishing behaviour this evening.

Every mortifying detail.

Wiping her eyes, she shot a guilty sideways glance towards Gabe, half expecting to see the dreadful wine stains on his white shirt. But all evidence was gone and she realised he'd had a wash and changed his shirt before they left Wattle Park.

'Gabe,' she said quickly, before she lost her nerve, 'I haven't apologised for tossing that wine over you.'

Without taking his eyes from the road, he shrugged. 'I guess I deserved it.'

Did he? Funny how quickly her feelings could change. Hugging her arms for warmth, she peered through the window at the rushing moonlit paddocks. This evening in the restaurant she'd been livid in her fury. And now...

How could one man have the power to disturb and anger her so profoundly and yet soothe and support her so beautifully?

Right now she was feeling comforted and very grateful for his company. Nevertheless... 'You were teasing Charles behind his back,' she said. 'And that was very rude.'

'I apologise.'

The words sounded sincere enough, but she thought she could see a smile twitching the corners of his mouth.

'We've both apologised so now we're even,' he added, and as they rounded the next curve he asked, 'I take it you really like the guy?'

She opened her mouth to respond and then shut it. What was the point in discussing Charles? The subject had closed when he'd hightailed it out of the restaurant after her shrewish performance.

Besides, she didn't want to examine her feelings for Charles while Michael was so much a part of her thoughts. Her grandfather wouldn't think much of him.

She tried to imagine bringing Charles home to Windaroo and introducing him to Michael. She pictured the three of them sitting down to dinner.

Oh, crumbs. She almost giggled as she saw a sudden vision of Charles explaining to a stunned Michael about the significance of volatile vapours released in a wine glass.

If only Grandad could trust her to look after Windaroo on her own she wouldn't have to worry about this whole marriage bit. Men were such a problem!

Last night at the ball she'd been pleased enough with Charles's pleasant kisses, but tonight his conversation had been a yawn.

'Piper?'

'Sorry. What did you ask?'

'This Kilgour fellow,' he muttered. 'Are you really set on him?'

A negative answer would only make Gabe smug again. 'I think Charles has many admirable qualities,' she said airily.

'That sounds like a comment from a schoolteacher writing a reference, not a girlfriend.'

'Well...he's also cute.'

*'Cute?'*

'Yes.' Wasn't that how she'd heard the girls in Mullinjim describe their boyfriends?

'So that's what you want to run Windaroo? Someone *cute*?'

'Yeah, a cute cattleman,' she said. 'Sounds perfect.'

'Perfectly ludicrous.'

The sudden beeping from Gabe's phone banished any thoughts of Charles and sent chill dread flooding through Piper.

Gabe's face was grim as he pulled over to the side of the highway to take the call.

*Oh, Grandad, please be OK. Please!*

But she could read the bad news in the awful tightening of Gabe's face and the way his throat worked.

His shoulders slumped as he depressed the button on his phone and a sob broke from her throat. 'He—he's gone, isn't he?'

Gabe's eyes gleamed damply as he nodded. ''Fraid so, kitten.'

An agonising, horrible blackness filled her chest, brewed around her heart and welled upwards to her throat. 'Oh—oh—oh—G-Gabe.'

Without another word he reached for her, and she lunged towards him, falling against him, unable to hold back the great noisy, gasping sobs that shook her whole body.

Oh, how could she bear this? This sudden gaping cavern of loneliness? This awful, awful black emptiness?

Her poor, darling grandfather. Gone.

She was shaking as Gabe gathered her close. 'I'm so sorry,' he murmured as he drew her head against his big, comforting chest. His fingers stroked her hair and his gentle lips brushed against her forehead as he made soft, soothing noises.

And he let her cry.

# CHAPTER ELEVEN

AFTER the funeral, everyone gathered in the hall next to the church for refreshments. Piper was exhausted. Wearing her black dress, and with her hair carefully braided, she stood in one corner of the room, holding a cup of cooling tea while she greeted a stream of people and accepted their condolences. She felt vaguely disorientated, as if she were watching the scene from afar.

She hadn't been able to sleep or eat properly for days. Her mind had been a feverish blur of unhappiness, decisions to be made about the service, phone calls and well-meaning visitors.

Then, in between all the busyness, there had been times of awful, awful loneliness.

'Excuse me, Piper?'

She turned towards the voice and found Jim Holmes, her grandfather's solicitor, standing at her elbow. A small man, with a fringe of grey hair circling his pate and a tiny grey moustache, Jim looked perpetually worried. 'I need to have a word with you soon,' he said. 'I want to explain about your grandfather's will.'

'Oh, yes, of course.' Quite unexpectedly, her heartbeats began a nervous pounding. She hadn't been allowing herself to think about the future. About what might happen to Windaroo now. Grandad had been so against leaving her to run the property on her own, and she had no idea how things stood.

There was every chance she was about to lose her home!

'Tomorrow morning in my office?' Jim suggested. 'Nine o'clock?'

'Yes,' she replied, feeling strangely hollow and uneasy. Her teeth chewed her lower lip. There were so many questions she suddenly wanted to ask him, but now was hardly the time. She would have to be patient. Another sleepless night!

As Jim moved away again she felt someone tug at her braid from behind and, turning around, discovered Gabe. Her face lit with pleasure to find him so near.

'I know just what you need,' he said.

Her heart gave a strange little lift. 'What's that?'

'An hour on the creek bank at dusk with a fishing rod in your hand.'

'Oh, yes!' she cried, delighted. 'That would be wonderful. Let's do it.' Trust Gabe to understand exactly how she was feeling. 'You're an angel, Gabriel.' Heavens, she hadn't used that old joke in years.

'I'll bring a frying pan so we can cook what we catch.'

Her smile broadened. 'We may as well be optimistic.'

As he moved off again she wished she could feel as hopeful about her future on Windaroo.

The black bream weren't biting.

'We might as well be fishing for bunyips,' Gabe complained as he sprawled on the creek bank beside his abandoned fishing rod and watched the fading sunlight drip like melted butter through the slender, tapered leaves of the eucalypts.

Piper was sitting higher up the bank, with her back against the sun-warmed trunk of a paperbark, but now she bent forward, an inquisitive smile teasing her lips. 'I've always been curious about bunyip fishing. I mean, everyone knows bunyips don't exist except in aboriginal legends, but I was dreadfully jealous that you and Jonno would go fishing for them and never let me come. What were you really doing?'

Gabe tipped his head further back so that he was looking at her upside down. 'You were too young to come with us—and anyway, you've never liked beer.'

'What's beer got to do with it?'

Rolling onto his side, he propped his head on his hand and grinned at her. 'This is secret men's business, but just this once I'll let you in on the inside story.'

'I'm excessively flattered.' She made an exaggerated show of rolling her eyes to hide how pleased she was. 'Do tell.'

'Well, the theory is that bunyips like hot beer. So, when you're fishing for them, you tie a hot beer on the end of your line. But after a beer has spent half an hour lying on the bottom of a creek it gets too cold, so you have to take it out and put another hot one on the line.'

'And of course it makes sense to drink the coldie.'

'Of course.'

Piper laughed. 'So that's why you guys always came back half tanked from bunyip fishing trips.'

He grinned, but the smile faded as he looked off into the distance. 'Haven't been bunyip fishing for years.'

'Well, you haven't been in the bush, have you, Captain Rivers? You've been away conquering the skies and being a hero.'

Gabe didn't answer. Instead, he reached over to the canvas pack he'd brought with him and said, 'I kind of expected the fish might be off the bite, so I came prepared with some sausages. Want to cook them up instead?'

'Mmm.' She hadn't eaten all day, and the thought of

frying sausages sent her tastebuds into a sudden whirl of anticipation. She licked her lips.

Then she saw the way Gabe's eyes followed the movement of her tongue. There was an unnerving wariness in his gaze, as if he was having second thoughts about being down here—alone with her on a creek bank. Was he thinking what she was thinking? About that incredible kiss they'd shared?

Neither she nor Gabe looked away.

Trapped by his green eyes, she could feel her blood beating at every pulse-point in her body.

At last he pulled his gaze away. 'Better look for some firewood before it gets too dark,' he said, and jumped to his feet.

'Sure.' Her stomach felt weightless and jittery as she wound in her fishing line.

While they gathered branches and twigs the tropical night closed in with its usual swiftness, the light changing quickly from golden to mauve, then deepening and spreading shadows. By the time their little campfire was blazing it was quite dark.

Their sausages smelled sensational as they sizzled in the pan. And they tasted even better. Gabe speared them with gum tree twigs and they sat cross-legged and ate them from the twigs, grinning and licking their lips and fingers like hungry children.

'I'd forgotten how good a sausage on a stick can taste,' Piper said between munches.

'Nothing quite like it, is there?'

'Except for my raisin damper, dripping with golden syrup. Remember when I used to make that?' She shot him a quick sideways smile.

'Yeah. I must admit you've always had quite a way with bush tucker.'

She sensed that they were both trying to find a way back to their old, comfortable relationship. But there was a new awkwardness, an unnerving awareness getting in the way.

Once again their gazes caught and held. While her heart went crazy. While their little fire crackled and snapped. While her smile faded as his deep green eyes searched her face and her body grew tight and warm with the memory of his kiss.

Memory of the magic, the explosive impact of finding her body jammed against his. Her breasts pressed against his hard muscles. His strong arms binding her. And then his mouth! Oh, man! His lips, warm with want, moving over hers, pushing hers apart so he could taste her. Gabe. Lovely Gabe. Sending her dizzy! Making her burn! Making her think about falling in love.

Help! What she had to remember was the aftermath! His humiliating reaction!

'Look,' Gabe said, suddenly breaking into her thoughts, 'do you want me to ring Charles Kilgour?'

She almost fell into the fire with shock and disappointment. 'Why would you want to do that?'

He avoided her gaze and stared into the flickering flames. 'I could set things straight for you. I know I annoyed the hell out of you last weekend, and I really cruelled your chances with the guy.'

'Oh…' She tried to cover her confusion by using her twig to scratch a circle in the dirt.

'I was over-protective and interfering,' he said.

'Yes, you were.'

'But I can make up a cover story about what happened and set something up for you two to be together again.'

*Great!*

What a fool she was. A minute ago she'd been thinking about kissing Gabe again and now he was calmly discussing Charles. Stinging tears of frustration seeped beneath her eyelids. She shaded her eyes with one hand and batted at smoke with the other, hoping the pretence would convince Gabe that the fire was the problem. Not *him.*

What would he think if she admitted that she would never have looked twice at Charles if Gabe had—

Holy mackerel! Her heart thumped like a trapped wild thing. The truth caught her like a fisherman's hook, reeling her in, gasping and spluttering with shock. She was in love with Gabe. Totally, hopelessly in love.

Oh, heavens, no. How silly of her. He'd always been a god-like kind of super-hero for her, but she'd never let herself think of him as a lover! But now she couldn't think of anything else! She closed her eyes to hold back the rush of tears.

Twigs snapped under his weight as he leaned towards her, and she felt his hand cupping her chin.

'Piper?' he whispered.

If she opened her eyes he would see her tears. *Oh, Gabe, what am I going to do? Can't you guess how I feel?* Oh, why was life so complicated?

'Piper?' Gabe repeated, tilting her chin towards him. 'What's the matter?'

'Nothing.'

She couldn't open her eyes. She didn't dare let him see her embarrassing secret. Her heart was drumming; her skin was on fire. She wanted so much for him to kiss her again.

'If this is about Charles, I'm really very sorry,' he said. 'I had no right to invade your territory like that.'

Oh, why couldn't he forget about Charles?

'Don't worry about it,' she cried loudly.

'But you're so upset. My behaviour was unforgivable. It's—it's just hard for me to get out of the habit of protecting you.' His thumb stroked her cheek, once, twice. 'Hey,' he said as he encountered an errant tear. 'Hey, Piper, you're really upset.'

She shook her head, unable to speak. Any minute now she would make a complete fool of herself and start sobbing her eyes out.

'Look, if you'd like me to hang around for a while I don't have to rush off to Sydney straight away,' he said.

Her eyes flashed open. 'Sydney?'

He was looking at her with a funny-sad, puzzled smile. Her heart did a loop-the-loop.

'I have to get back there at some stage, to start planning my future, but if you need an escort to take you to more parties so you can meet more guys I'm your man,' he said. 'I promise I won't interfere like last time.'

'Oh, for crying out loud!' She sniffed, pulling away from him and swiping at her eyes.

Why was he so intent on foisting her onto other men? How could he be so sensitive to so many of her needs and yet so ignorant of her most glaring need? And why, oh, why, had he kissed her so passionately the other night when he didn't really want her at all?

'I'm not going to any more balls or parties,' she shouted as she pushed herself to her feet. 'I don't give a stuff about getting married. And if I did, I certainly wouldn't need your help.'

'OK, OK! I get the message.' In one fluid motion he jumped to his feet and reached out to take her arm.

'Don't touch me.' She wrenched away from his grasp. 'I've had enough of men.' She took a hasty step backwards and her boot slid over a piece of firewood. It rolled from under her, sending her toppling sideways.

Gabe caught her. And there she was. Imprisoned in his arms again, with her breasts squeezed against his powerful chest and her stomach hard against the rough denim of his jeans. She could feel the pounding of his heart, racing as hard as hers.

He clasped her tightly to him and she heard a deep, painful sound in his throat. Green fire smouldered in his eyes. *I think he wants to kiss me.*

Her breathing snagged, then seemed to stop altogether. *Do it, Gabe. Please.* If only she dared to ask him to kiss her again.

Go with your heart, Grandad had said. Maybe she should take a risk and kiss him?

But he was releasing her already, letting his hands slide slowly down her arms until only their fingertips were touching. 'You've had a huge day,' he said, tapping his fingers lightly against hers. 'You should get home.'

'Yes,' she sighed, feeling empty and aching and totally confused.

The moment was gone. There was nothing more to say, so she bent away from him and picked up the frying pan, wrapped it in a sheet of newspaper and shoved it into his pack. When she'd finished, she said, 'Tomorrow morning I've got to see Jim Holmes to find out about Grandad's will.' She ran a weary hand through her hair. 'I'm not looking forward to it.'

'Let me know if I can help in any way,' he said, and his eyes seemed to scorch her. But he said no more, simply turned away and began to kick dirt over the embers of their fire.

Gabe was in Edenvale's office making a phone call to Sydney when he heard the car door slam. Still holding the receiver to his ear, he stepped closer to the window to see who had arrived.

Piper.

She must have driven straight from the solicitor's office. One glance at her face as she marched across the front drive told him she was beyond upset.

'Excuse me, I'll have to call you back,' he said to the surprised aircraft salesman on the other end of the line. 'We have an emergency here.'

As he lowered the receiver, he grimaced. He'd been afraid something like this might happen. There'd always been a good chance that Michael Delaney's will would hold disturbing news for Piper.

And she'd come straight to him.

The way she always had when she was a kid—when her dog had died from snake bite, when she'd been scared about going away to boarding school, when she'd been mad at Michael for not letting her compete in a rodeo, or when he'd refused permission for her to have a tattoo.

As he headed for the front door Gabe smiled at those memories. Piper had always been so grateful for any little snippet of advice or comfort he'd thrown her way and she'd made him feel wise beyond his years. What a joke! His recent attempts to help her had proved what a jackass he really was.

At least assisting her to sort out some kind of legal issue should be a hell of a lot less complicated than getting involved in her love life. He'd spent far too many sleepless nights thinking about the complete hash he'd made of supervising her search for a husband—including that crazy, mind-blowing kiss!

He met her at the top of the steps.

She was looking sophisticated and businesslike in a

city-style suit—a neat blue jacket and short skirt with matching pumps. But there was nothing sophisticated about her demeanour. Red-faced, hands on hips and with blue eyes blazing, she greeted him with, 'You're not going to believe what Grandad's done!'

'Then you'd better come inside and tell me,' he answered, keeping his voice deliberately calm.

She didn't move, except to cast an anxious glance towards the interior of the house. Her braided hair was a splash of pale gold in the sunlight and Gabe only just resisted the impulse to reach out and touch it.

'Perhaps I'd better stay out here. I don't want to drag the rest of your family into this,' she said.

'My parents and Jonno are away at a cattle sale in Charters Towers today. We've got the place to ourselves.'

To his surprise she still hesitated, an uncharacteristic caution creeping into her eyes, but then she gave a little shake and squared her shoulders. 'OK. Thanks.'

Gabe took her into the lounge room, where she perched on the very edge of the deep, comfy chair he offered her. Her skirt didn't reach her knees and she kept her hands clenched at its hem.

He sat opposite and lounged back in an intentionally relaxed sprawl. 'I take it you're not happy with Michael's decisions about the future of the property?'

She inhaled deeply. 'You bet I'm not.' Turning her head to the side, she seemed to have trouble going on. She squeezed her eyes tightly shut and compressed her lips, as if she was trying to hold her feelings in check, and Gabe did his best to quash his growing uneasiness.

'It might be best if you just tell me the worst news first,' he suggested.

Her eyes flashed open and she stared at him hard.

'OK. Get this. Grandad's prepared to sell Windaroo to Karl Findley.'

'Findley? The cattle duffer?'

'Yup.'

That was the end of Gabe's relaxed sprawl. No wonder Piper was so upset. Hell. *He* was upset. 'Didn't Michael know we're almost certain that Findley's been taking your cattle?'

'Of course he knew. I made a huge song and dance about it. But the place is going to auction and he's known for ages that Findley shows every sign of being the highest bidder.'

'But the proceeds will still go to you?'

'Yes, but how awful is that, Gabe? How can I live with money I gained from selling Windaroo off to a swine like Findley? I don't want to sell Windaroo at all, but I can't bear the thought of handing it over to him!'

Gabe shook his head. 'Is this definite, Piper? There's no way out?'

She shifted restlessly and drew a pattern on the arm of her chair with her forefinger. 'Well...there are conditions.'

'What sort of conditions?'

Slumping back into the chair, she kept her eyes downcast as she said, 'Windaroo won't need to be sold at all if I'm married within a month of Grandad's death.'

# CHAPTER TWELVE

'CAN you believe my own grandfather would do this to me? He knew I have a snowflake in hell's chance of getting myself married inside a month.'

Piper watched Gabe's reaction to her news. She knew he was trying to appear calm, but she didn't miss the sudden clenching of his fists, the backwards thrust of his shoulders and the wary glint in his eyes.

He cleared his throat. 'I do know that Michael was very worried about leaving you with the huge responsibility of running the property on your own.'

'But I've been more or less looking after the place by myself for the past few years anyhow. I know it's not as productive as it could be, but it's not *that* bad.'

It was so unfair! The only reason she hadn't been able to improve Windaroo into a top producing property was because she'd been so preoccupied with her grandfather's failing health she hadn't been able to run the place as efficiently as she would have liked.

'Michael mentioned something to me once about debts,' Gabe said.

'Yes.' She let out a noisy sigh. 'Jim Holmes did explain about the overdue land taxes and the loan repayments Grandad took out some years back for improvements. But that doesn't mean he has to sell to *Karl Findley*!' She thumped the arm of the chair. 'I can't bear the thought of that man getting his grubby thieving hands on my land. My home!'

Gabe's eyes were troubled as he sat staring at the carpet square in the middle of the room and rubbed his chin thoughtfully. 'I suppose you could take the matter to the Public Trustee and the Courts, but it might take a lot of money and a long time to resolve.'

'Yeah. And according to Jim Holmes I don't really have enough money to consider that option.'

'So you still need to get married.'

She gave a little snort of disgust. 'No way. I've scrapped that idea. Once bitten and all that. I have absolutely no intention of spending the next month chasing around the countryside in search of a husband.'

A fleeting grin crossed his face. 'An outback Cinderella in search of Prince Charming.'

She smiled weakly. 'With a riding boot instead of a glass slipper? No, thank you.'

He startled her by leaping to his feet and striding away down the length of the room till he came to a halt in front of a window. With his back to her, he stood staring out across the verandah to the horse paddock and the stables.

'I'm going to look more closely into taking the issue to the Public Trustee,' Piper said, lifting her voice to reach him.

Gabe didn't respond. He stood at the window, apparently lost in thought, with his hands shoved so deeply into the back pockets of his faded jeans that his big shoulders strained the seams of his light cotton shirt.

'Gabe?'

He turned slowly and the searing, soul-piercing look in his eyes sent her heart thrumming.

She shifted in the chair, feeling suddenly uncomfortable, and tried to smile. But the smile faded before it was fully formed. Perhaps she'd gone too far. Here she was foisting yet another of her problems onto Gabe, and yet the guy had enough problems of his own. He'd come home to recuperate and regroup. He'd already indicated that any day now he would want to push off again to Sydney to get on with his own life…with his own women.

Pushing herself out of the chair, she stood facing him, rubbing her hands together nervously. 'Look…I'm sorry to land all this on you. I shouldn't have come rushing straight over here to blow off steam.'

*I just happen to be hopelessly in love with you and you're in my head twenty-four/seven and it seemed perfectly natural to…*

She blinked and bent down to pick up the shoulder bag she'd dumped on the floor beside her chair.

'You could always marry me.'

The strap of her bag slipped from nerveless fingers. Her knees turned to water and she had to grip the arm of the chair for support. Slowly she craned her head upwards to look across the room to him, and her heart flipped to see the intense look on his face. 'What did you say?' she asked faintly.

His mouth twisted into a crooked half-smile. 'I just proposed marriage, Piper.'

Oh, God. Her heart was pounding in her ears, but she *had* heard him correctly. Twice.

She almost gave in to her instinct to shout yes!

*Yes, yes, yes, Gabe!*

To throw her arms around him and scream, I'd love to marry you.

Except…except…painful, vexing common sense told her that Gabe had been listening to her babble on about needing a husband for weeks now and he'd had ample opportunity to propose before if he'd really wanted to. Lord help her! He was just being Gabe. Doing the right thing. He hadn't proposed marriage because he was in love with her. He was doing it because he knew how much Windaroo meant to her.

*Wake up, Piper. He's feeling sorry for you.*

He's just trying to protect you, like he always has.

How embarrassing!

'Thanks,' she said shakily. 'But—ah—' Oh, Lord, did she really have to say this? 'No, thanks.'

His jaw thrust to a formidable angle.

Man, why did he have to be so gorgeous? Why did she have to love every scrumptious bit of him? His dark hair kept military-style short. The crinkle lines around his eyes. The tiny scar making a skin-coloured track through his right eyebrow. The snug fit of his jeans. His willingness to listen to her rattling on about her worries…

He'd always been an important part of her life and right now her life seemed to be collapsing all around her.

The thought of Gabe as her husband was almost too wonderful to contemplate. Perhaps she should quickly change her mind? Perhaps she should just seize this unexpected gift from the gods—say yes and make him hers before he changed *his* mind.

*If only… If only he wasn't making this offer for all the wrong reasons. If only he loved her.*

A week ago she might have said yes, anyhow, just because it would be so damn good to have Gabe all to herself. But a week ago she'd still been blind to the truth. She hadn't realised just how deeply and irrevocably she loved him.

Now she knew that being married to Gabe would be like a slow, painful, torturous death because he didn't love her back.

'You're not thinking straight,' she told him sharply. 'You don't mean it.' He hadn't touched her, hadn't said one word about love.

'I'm certainly not joking, Piper.'

'It would be a terrible mistake,' she said, sounding much braver than she felt.

'Why?'

A corner of her mouth quirked upwards. 'You've been watching me make a fool of myself while I've hunted around for a husband and you've never once suggested that I could marry *you.*'

His eyes took on a haunted, puzzled look.

'You haven't, have you, Gabe?'

'No.'

He took a deep breath, then fell silent, and the tiny bubble of hope in her chest fizzled.

'Why are you offering now?' She spun away quickly, hoping he wouldn't see the tremble in her chin. 'Forget I asked that. I know why.'

Behind her she heard his footsteps coming across the polished oak floor, then he stopped close by and her breath caught as she waited for his touch. But it didn't come.

'I think we could make a go of it,' he said softly.

A groan escaped. His noble sense of duty scythed a painful slash deep inside her. 'Make a go of it?' she echoed, her voice high and brittle with emotion. 'I don't want a marriage that sounds like hard work before we even start.'

'I didn't mean to sound negative, but if you look at it sensibly—'

Whirling around, she held up shaking hands to ward him off. 'Don't say any more, Gabe. You're making this worse.'

His beautiful mouth thinned as his eyes studied her silently.

'I know you want to help me, but I'll be OK, Gabe.'

'But you have so much to deal with—losing Michael and now Windaroo.'

There it was. Absolute evidence that he was doing this out of pity. 'Don't you remember? You told me once before I shouldn't choose a husband out of desperation. Thanks for that advice. You were right.' Her chin lifted. 'I'd rather lose Windaroo to Karl Findley than accept your offer.'

Ducking to avoid his surprised gaze, she reached down to retrieve her dropped shoulder bag.

When she straightened she was struggling to hold back tears, but she took one great gulping breath and found the courage to add, 'Let *me* give *you* one little piece of advice, Captain Rivers. You might be the expert when it comes to flirting and kissing and sex, but when it comes to proposing marriage you don't know diddly-squat. No self-respecting girl can accept a marriage proposal from a man who asks her from the other side of the room.'

Then, before she made a complete fool of herself by bursting into tears, she rushed out of the door. He called to her once, but she didn't turn back.

She hurried down the front steps towards her ute, her

face puckered with the effort of holding back sobs. As she crossed the drive her silly heart kept hoping that he would come running after her, that at any moment she would hear him cry out, *Wait, Piper. You don't understand. I really love you.*

She reached the ute, wrenched the door open, scrambled into the driver's seat and thrust the keys into the ignition. There was no sound or sight of Gabe.

Her back wheels spun out embarrassing sprays of gravel as her foot hit the accelerator and she shot down Edenvale's drive.

Twenty-four weary hours later, Gabe found his mother in Edenvale's kitchen, her hands covered in flour as she kneaded bread dough. She looked up when she heard his footsteps, her ready smile automatically in place. But her smile faded when she saw the duffel bag slung over his shoulder.

'Are you heading off again?'

He lowered the bag to the floor and stood awkwardly with his hands shoved into his pockets. 'Yes. I need to get back to Sydney to start sorting a few things out.'

Dropping her gaze to the soft ball of dough, Eleanor punched into it with a closed fist. 'I thought you were still sorting out a few things here.'

'All sorted,' he said.

'I see,' she said quietly, and the sharp green flash in her eyes signalled to Gabe that perhaps she saw a little more than he would have liked. 'Have you mentioned your plans to your father?'

'I told him I've decided to buy a helicopter. I want to set up my own chopper mustering company.'

'And you'll be using Edenvale as your home base?'

'Perhaps,' he admitted, bringing one hand up to scratch the back of his neck. 'But I might be better off using a bigger centre, like Charters Towers or even Townsville. They're the sorts of things I need to research.'

His mother watched him thoughtfully, then her mouth pulled into a grimacing smile as she moved to the sink to wash the flour from her hands. 'It's probably a good thing that you're taking off for a while.'

'Glad you think so.'

'Some distance will give you a chance to get a better perspective on—what's been happening here.'

He frowned. 'What do you mean? There's nothing happening of any importance. I don't need any kind of perspective.'

'Oh, Gabe,' Eleanor said with an impatient sigh. 'I know you're too old for me to pry, but you've been fussing and fretting around Piper O'Malley like a frustrated rooster.'

*'Rooster?'* Gabe cried, shocked by his mother's bluntness.

'Yes, dear.'

'I can't believe I'm hearing this from my own mother.'

She met his accusing gaze with steely tolerance. 'Normally I wouldn't say boo about your affairs with women.'

'You're fantasising, Mother. There is no affair and I haven't been fretting and I certainly haven't been frustrated.'

*And what a load of old codswallop that was.*

His mother's eyebrows rose in a silent challenge. 'As I said, it'll be good for you to get back to Sydney. Roosters spend too much time scratching around in the dust. From far away you might get more of an eagle's eye view on your situation and work out what you really want.'

Sighing wearily, Gabe shook his head. 'Well…thanks for the psychological insights, Mum.' He stepped forward, threw an arm across her shoulders and kissed her cheek, and then from out of nowhere found himself speaking with unexpected honesty. 'Actually, if you must know I feel more like an old feather duster than a rooster.'

'Oh, darling,' she murmured, wrapping sympathetic arms around him and hugging him tight. 'You make sure you hurry right back here the very minute you've sorted everything out.'

Time was a strange phenomenon, Piper decided. A month could drag on interminably when you were feeling utterly miserable and yet, when you never wanted it to end, that same month could also rush by with the speed of light.

She spent the next four weeks in an extended, miserable blur. After she consulted the banks and the Public Trustee she discovered that she couldn't afford to contest her grandfather's will, and so, heartsick at the thought of leaving, she permitted auction signs to be nailed on Windaroo's gates. She mustered the cattle, organised somewhere for her books and furniture to be stored and found a new home for Roy.

Four weeks of heartbreak…of missing her grandfather…of travelling all over the property, trying to shore up memories. Four weeks of missing Gabe…

He'd left for the coast the day after she'd rejected his offer. And she hadn't heard from him since.

She and Roy kept up the tradition of sharing afternoon tea in Windaroo's homey, old-fashioned kitchen. They wore very stiff upper lips and were strictly practical as they discussed their futures and what needed to be done around the property. Piper didn't want to worry Roy, so she didn't air any of the questions that were ricocheting back and forth in her head like maddened wasps trapped in a jam jar. But she longed to.

At afternoon tea on the day before Windaroo was to be auctioned, he pushed a plate of iced biscuits towards her. 'You're losing weight, girlie,' he said. 'Come on, eat one of these for my sake. You've got to get your appetite back.'

She picked up the biscuit and held it halfway to her mouth, but the thought of eating made her feel ill. Placing it back, she picked up her cup of tea instead. 'I can't eat right now, Roy. I just can't.'

Roy frowned. 'I'm worried about you, Piper.'

'I'll be OK once I get tomorrow out of the way.' Next moment her cup clattered against the saucer. 'Oh, Roy, why did Grandad do this to us? I can't believe he wanted us both to lose Windaroo. And to a cattle duffer! The auctioneer still thinks Karl Findley will offer the highest bid tomorrow.'

Roy sighed. 'It's a sad, sorry thing, all right.'

'And I can't believe Grandad wanted you to head off to a retirement home in Charters Towers.' She covered her face with trembling hands.

'He didn't.'

The certainty in his voice forced her to peek at him over the tops of her fingers. 'What do you mean?'

'Michael knew if you stayed on here you'd let me stay here, too.'

'Yes, but he made it impossible for me to stay here.'

Roy folded his arms and rested them on the table. Leaning towards her, he spoke softly out of the side of his mouth, as if he were afraid someone might overhear him. 'He really expected you to be married by now. That's what he wanted.'

'But how could he?' Piper cried. 'He knew a girl can't just hang up a sign and get herself married off in a matter of weeks.'

'I reckon he thought you'd be married to Gabe.'

Bells clanged in her head, making her temples throb. 'You're joking.' A fine sheen of sweat filmed her and she was suddenly cold.

'No. He was fair dinkum,' Roy said with a sad shake of his head. 'I tried to tell him that he might have the wrong end of the stick, but he reckoned you two were a match made in heaven. All you needed was a wake-up call to realise how you felt about each other.'

'When did he tell you this?'

'Ages ago, when Gabe was inviting you over to Wattle Park.'

Piper blinked back burning tears. 'Why didn't Grandad talk it over with me? I could have set him straight.'

Roy shrugged. 'Michael thought he had it all sorted out. He reckoned that even if you didn't get married before he died, as soon as Gabe heard the conditions of his will he'd propose to you and everything would be hunky-dory.'

'Oh.'

Roy's words struck like brutal blows to an unhealed wound.

'Mind you,' Roy added, 'I told him that he was being too subtle. I reckon if you want someone to get a message you gotta make it real clear. Call a spade a shovel.' He shot her a cautious frown. 'Obviously Gabe missed the message, or he wouldn't have cleared off the way he did.'

*Oh, he got the message all right.*

She sank her head into her hands. How many times in the past four weeks had she wondered if she'd been completely mad to reject Gabe? The man she loved had asked her to marry him and she'd said no.

No doubt her grandfather would have thought she was crazy. She sighed loudly. Men were the pits! How could they be so *dense*? Didn't any of them understand that there was more to marriage than a property settlement?

Heavens, it was Michael who'd told her to use her heart not her head when she chose a husband! Couldn't he understand that was Gabe's prerogative too? When a man proposed to a woman it should be because he truly loved her, not because he felt sorry for her.

She'd gone over the scene when Gabe proposed a million times. And for another million she'd wondered what might have happened if she'd stayed and given him a chance to explain his offer. She'd even gone so far as imagining that perhaps Gabe did love her but hadn't admitted it—not even to himself. Perhaps she was so inexperienced and insecure that she'd never given him any of the right signals and he hadn't felt free to admit his true feelings?

And then at other times she was quite sure that her

first reaction had been spot-on. Gabe didn't love her. Not the marrying kind of love. He merely felt sorry for her.

No matter which way she looked at it she could never find an answer that offered any comfort—because, although she was sure she'd done the right thing, she suspected that her refusal had somehow violated their friendship. And that felt like death.

Her chair scraped on the pine floorboards as she rose and took their empty cups to the sink. After she rinsed them she stood leaning against the sink, watching the water drain down the plughole. That was how she felt—as if she were draining away, disappearing into a bottomless black hole. That was how she saw her future now.

Of course in stronger moments she had plans to start again. With the money from Windaroo she could buy another property—something modest, within her means—and she could select a small herd and start again from scratch. Some days she even looked forward to the challenge. But today she felt too flattened, too miserably aware that she had lost the only property she'd ever really wanted. She'd lost everything she'd ever loved…

In one fell swoop her grandfather, Windaroo and Gabe were gone and her life looked like one gaping black hole of nothingness.

'What's that sound?' Roy asked.

She shrugged, unwilling to admit to him that she hadn't been hearing anything except the misery in her own head. But as she hung a damp teatowel on the rack behind the door she cocked her head to one side and listened.

At first she only heard the wind rattling a loose piece of iron in the tractor shed, but then from far off came a faint thud-thud-thudding sound. 'You've got good hearing for an old cobber,' she said with a faint grin. 'Could be a helicopter.'

Roy nodded. 'Coming back from doing a muster, I guess.' He grimaced as he rose from his chair. His arthritis seemed worse these days and he had to take his time getting to his feet. 'I'll be off, then, Piper. Thanks for the cuppa. Now, you won't be too morbid alone here tonight, will you?'

She patted his shoulder. 'Don't worry about me, mate.'

About to hobble off, Roy paused and looked through the window to the sky beyond. 'That chopper's coming over this way.'

'Is it?'

She listened once more and the sound of the motor was definitely getting louder. It was more of a throbbing crack-crack-crack now. Following the direction of his gaze, she realised that, yes, a helicopter was swooping low over Windaroo's paddocks.

Sudden excitement danced in Roy's eyes. 'It's going to land here.'

Goosebumps broke out on Piper's arms. Her stomach turned fluttery with nerves. With a roaring clatter-clatter-clatter, the helicopter dropped the final few metres into the paddock beyond the tractor shed, and her knees wobbled so that she had to lean against the sink for support.

The whirlwind created by the chopper's down-draught sent dust and dried grass flying above the shed's roof.

'I wonder who it is,' Roy said. 'My hearing might be OK but my eyesight's not much chop.'

'I don't know,' Piper whispered. She'd caught a brief

glimpse of the pilot and had time to notice that he was a man with dark hair before the shed blocked her view.

'Might be Gabe,' Roy added, and his eyes lit up with sudden excitement.

'It can't be him; he's in Sydney,' she snapped, but just the thought that it might possibly be Gabe filled her with harrowing, joyful, mind-numbing alarm.

'What are you waiting for? Go and find out who it is, girl.'

She shot Roy a puzzled glance. The urgency in the old man's voice was so unlike him. 'I suppose I should,' she said, and raised shaking hands to tuck stray strands of hair behind her ears. She'd hardly glanced in a mirror of late and she probably looked a fright.

Her legs felt like trembling jelly as she stepped out onto the verandah. If this visitor was Gabe, she couldn't imagine what he was doing here.

She wasn't sure how she made it down the steps and across the stretch of lawn to the paddock's bush timber gate. The helicopter stood in the middle of the paddock. Its rotorblades had almost stopped spinning, and as she fumbled with the gate chain she saw the pilot climbing down from the cabin. Long legs in faded jeans that rode low over slim hips… Her heart stumbled. It was Gabe. No man wore jeans quite the way he did.

He stepped out, away from the chopper, and waved to her. She saw his dark hair, a little longer than before, his flashing smile, wide shoulders, a blue shirt with long sleeves rolled up to just beneath his elbows. Gabe. Home.

Why?

Why today?

Her mind boiled—one second urging her to run to

greet him, the next telling her to run clear in the opposite direction. Heavens, she was wearing her oldest patched jeans and an ancient pink T-shirt that had been washed so many times it was as thin as nylon.

And why was she having so much trouble with the blasted gate? She'd opened it practically every day of her life. It was a simple matter of unhooking a link of iron chain. But her hands were shaking and her eyes were blurred and her heart was pounding and…

At last the hook came away and the gate creaked open. Ankle-high grass swished against her riding boots as she crossed the paddock.

Gabe was striding briskly towards her with no sign of a limp, and he reached her before she made it halfway. They both stopped at the same moment and stood stock-still a metre or so apart.

'Hi,' he said softly.

'Hi.'

Neither of them smiled and Piper could feel the awkwardness of their parting hanging between them like a force field. A gust of wind caught the collar of his shirt and flicked it up against his neck.

*What was he doing here? He'd gone back to his city life. Why had he returned here now?*

'How have you been?' he asked, his green eyes shadowed, unreadable.

'So-so.' She shrugged. 'Busy.'

His unsmiling gaze travelled over her, then he offered her a tiny half-smile and nodded his head in the helicopter's direction. 'Thought I'd drop in and show you my new toy.'

'It—it's beautiful.'

'I plan to start my own mustering service.'

'Where?'

He stood, loose-hipped, feet planted wide apart. 'Around here.'

'Oh.' The ground seemed to tilt beneath her. Tomorrow she would be leaving her home and Gabe was coming back. How ironic was that?

'Do you want to come for a quick joy ride?'

'Oh, I—' She dropped her gaze to her hands and saw that she was twisting them together. She slapped them to her sides.

It was just like Gabe to sweep back into her life and carry on as if nothing had changed. He'd been doing it for years, and each time she'd been thrilled to see him come back and devastated to see him go.

But in the past nothing much *had* changed, whereas now...

'I'm a very safe pilot,' he said, letting his mouth relax into a slow smile. 'I won't frighten you with any fancy tricks.' He held out one tanned hand to her, but she kept her own hands tightly at her sides.

The skin around his eyes crinkled and he smiled some more. 'Come on, Piper.'

Oh, she was weak. When he smiled at her like that she wanted to carry on as if nothing had changed, too. It was infinitely better than living in the awful empty loneliness of the past month. Besides, she'd spent a lot of time over the years trying to picture Gabe in a helicopter and the temptation to experience it for herself was too much. When he turned and strode back to the aircraft she followed.

Strapped into her seat, she looked in awe at the bank of instrument panels. 'There are so many dials and switches. How do you ever remember what to do with them all?'

He chuckled. 'This is a very simple little craft. You should have seen the inside of the Black Hawks I flew.'

'How much bigger were they?'

'Well, this craft only seats two max. In a Black Hawk we had a crew of three and we could lift an entire eleven-man fully equipped infantry squad, or take seats out to carry four litters.'

'And I suppose you had a lot of extra military gear as well?'

He nodded. 'We could fly at a hundred and sixty miles per hour, so we needed a lot more bells and whistles, but we also had a dispenser for infra-red jamming flares, mounting frames on the doors for machine guns—all that sort of stuff.'

She waved at the instruments in front of them. 'What are all these for?'

'Oh,' he said casually as he pointed to a row of dials, 'this is the altitude indicator. This is a low-airspeed indicator. Here we have fuel control, horizontal situation indicator, the torque metre.' As he rattled off the various names Piper saw the excited glow, the unmistakable pleasure and pride in his eyes.

This was a side of Gabe that she'd always wondered about but never known, never shared.

Then she saw something that made her heart stop.

Just above one of the dials. A wedge-tailed eagle made from beaten silver. She couldn't hold back her choked cry of surprise. It was the gift she'd given him when he was eighteen and had first gone away to join the army. 'You've still got the eagle.'

Gabe grinned as he tapped its silver beak lightly with

one finger. 'Of course. She was our mascot. My good luck charm. The guys in my crew wouldn't let me fly anywhere without her.'

'Really?' She'd had no idea. She took a deep, gulping breath. 'Are all mascots called she?'

The tips of Gabe's ears reddened. 'We—ah—the guys named this one after you, Piper.'

'Oh.'

Gabe had flown with her eagle. All those years. On every flight. It didn't mean anything. It couldn't mean anything—and yet—somehow—it seemed to mean *everything*.

'So, are you OK for take-off?' he asked.

She was shaking and fighting tears, and her stomach was churning, but somehow she replied, 'OK. All clear, Captain Rivers. I'm ready.'

He grinned. 'One joy ride coming up, ma'am.'

As the ground dropped away beneath them she sat tense and stiff in the seat, clutching her seat belt with her eyes pressed tightly shut against the stinging tears.

'Hey, Piper, you'll miss all the fun if you don't look.'

'I was feeling sick,' she said, but she forced her eyes open and was shocked to find how far above Windaroo she was already.

'I'll keep at a level height for a while. You should feel all right then.' Gabe shot her a frowning sideways glance. 'You *have* been looking after yourself, haven't you, fruit fly?'

'I'm fine,' she said, not meeting his gaze. She made a show of pointing at a windmill in the paddock below. 'That old thing's so rusty it's a wonder it still works.'

'The land's holding out pretty well, considering it hasn't rained since last wet season,' he said.

'Yes,' she agreed, and sighed. From up here, everything about her familiar world—the station buildings, the windmills, the turkey nest dam and the stockyards—looked so tiny they could have been plastic toys in a child's farm set.

Windaroo. Her world. And she was about to leave it—cast into exile.

What lousy timing Gabe had! How could she be expected to *enjoy* her joy ride today, of all days?

Below them, the gently rolling, pale gold Mitchell grass plains dotted with cattle looked like the sweetest, dearest sight on earth.

'I've never been able to understand how helicopters work,' she said, in an effort to stop thinking about everything she was about to lose.

And for the next few minutes she tried hard to concentrate while Gabe explained about rotor shafts, drive shafts, reciprocating gasoline engines and the way the tail rotor prevented the craft from spinning.

But she didn't take much in when below her stretched Windaroo and every corner was familiar. They flew over a patch of uncleared forest land towards the eastern boundary and she could see clouds of budgerigars wheeling over and through the trees.

From this altitude the foliage looked like one green mass, but she'd ridden through that bushland many times searching for straying cattle, and even from this height she could identify the subtle differences between the desert oaks, the bloodwoods and the ghost gums.

Oh, heavens! This was too hard! Her throat stung with gathering tears. She loved this place so much and it was her home for only a few more measly hours!

Gabe swooped back towards the west and followed

Mullinjim Creek till they reached the point where the main creek joined Little Mullinjim at Horseshoe Bend.

'Remember when we camped here?' he asked.

Oh, yes, she remembered too well. Years ago they had ridden their horses there with Jonno and spent a full week camped beside the water hole. From dawn till dusk they'd swum, fished and caught yabbies.

At night they'd sat around their campfire and cooked their fish, and Piper had mixed sweet damper dough studded with juicy raisins, which they'd wrapped around green sticks and held over the fire. And as they'd eaten the warm damper, dripping with rich golden syrup, they'd taken it in turns to freak each other out with ghost stories—about mad bushrangers and headless drovers. The rule had been that each story had to be more gruesome than the last.

It had been the most wonderful holiday of her life.

'Gabe, please!' she cried. 'Please, take me back!'

She couldn't bear it any longer. Flying over Windaroo today, she felt as if her whole life was flashing before her—as if these were the final seconds before she drowned. She was drowning now, drowning in memories, drowning in the hopelessness of it all. 'Why are you doing this?' she cried. 'Why are you forcing me to relive so many happy memories when you know I've got to give all of this up tomorrow?'

He shot one worried glance her way and without another word manoeuvred the helicopter so that it was heading back to the homestead. 'I'm sorry,' he said. 'I guess I just wanted to show off.' He looked for a moment as if he wanted to say more, but then decided against it.

They didn't speak as they flew back to the paddock

nearest the homestead. Piper sat hunched over, hugging her jittery stomach, fighting tears and telling herself she'd been a weak-willed wimp to come on this flight. If she'd had any backbone she would have congratulated Gabe on his purchase and told him she was far too busy preparing for the sale to joy ride with him.

'Sorry if you didn't enjoy that,' Gabe said as soon as they landed. His eyes were troubled as he looked at her. 'Flying can take a bit of getting used to.'

'It's not the flying that's bothering me,' she explained in a flat, weary voice. 'It's your timing. You know Windaroo is being auctioned tomorrow?'

A surprising deep flush darkened his face. 'Yes.'

As she stared at his heightened colour she felt suddenly compelled to say something about the way she'd run out on him. 'Gabe, I'm sorry I left so abruptly last time we—when you—when—' Oh, help! She couldn't get it out. What a mess!

'You were right, Piper,' he said smoothly. 'Your response was totally justified. I'm the one who should apologise.'

*Why? For not loving her?*

She looked away. Beyond the helicopter, afternoon shadows were creeping across the paddock. It would be night soon. Her last night before she lost Windaroo for ever. After tomorrow her life would never be the same.

A suffocating fog of despair and loneliness tinged with fear seemed to press in around her. If she was a drinker, she'd get herself well and truly blotto tonight.

If only she and Gabe could go back to the way they used to be.

Once, she wouldn't have hesitated to ask him to stay the night with her. Just as a friend, of course. And she knew he would have come to the auction to give her moral support.

She'd mucked up a wonderful friendship by falling in love with Gabe and wanting too much. Wanting him to be as crazily, hopelessly in love with her as she was with him.

She looked down at her hands, then up to the eagle perched above the bank of dials on the control panel, then back outside to the lengthening shadows.

'Thanks for the ride, Gabe.'

He nodded, but seemed preoccupied by other thoughts as she climbed out of the helicopter.

The afternoon was slipping towards dusk and the sun was flashing dark gold between distant tree trunks as she hurried across the paddock. When she reached the end of the paddock she realised she'd left the gate open. Fancy that! She never forgot to shut gates. *Shows what a mess I was in when Gabe arrived.*

Behind her she heard him start the motor, so she turned and gave the briefest little fluttering wave. But she didn't look again as the chopper lifted off and she crossed to the dark, empty homestead.

# CHAPTER THIRTEEN

THE auction was scheduled for eleven a.m.

At ten, Karl Findley and his wife arrived, and Mrs Findley made a tour of the house. She turned her nose up at the kitchen because it didn't have a dishwasher and was far too old-fashioned for her taste.

*Good.* Piper left them to it.

When Roy arrived, he frowned as he studied her white face and the deep shadows beneath her eyes—clear evidence that she hadn't slept at all last night. 'How are you?'

'Dreadful.' She dropped her gaze and inhaled deeply. 'I don't know if I can bear to sit through this.'

'You don't have to.'

'I do. I know it's going to be awful, but I have to see what happens. It would be worse if I ran away and hid and didn't know what was going on.'

'How's Gabe?' he asked.

'Fine.'

'Is he coming this morning?'

'I shouldn't think so,' she said in an icy tone she hoped would silence further questions. Then quickly she took Roy's hand. 'But it's so good of you to be here, old mate.'

He squinted at a cloud of dust rolling down the track. 'Looks like more people coming.'

'The auctioneer said quite a few people will turn up simply out of curiosity.'

'I s'pose they will.'

'Just under an hour to go,' she said, and let out a shaky sigh. 'I wish this could be over.'

They spent the next forty-five minutes sitting under the mango tree behind the house. Piper didn't want to go back into the house, where inspections were being made, or to wait on the front verandah where she might be expected to greet arrivals as if she were pleased to see them.

By the time eleven o'clock crawled around more than a dozen vehicles were lined up near the tractor shed. The auctioneer set out plastic chairs on the stretch of lawn shaded by the jacaranda near the front steps—the very spot where her parents had been married—and positioned himself up on the verandah, where he had a good view of everyone.

Karl Findley sat towards the front, nursing his beer belly and smirking smugly when he caught Piper's eye. Her fists curled with a fierce desire to smash his teeth in. His thin wife sat beside him, looking around at everyone with a shocked, nervous frown, as if she hadn't expected anyone else to turn up.

Piper and Roy sat towards the back of the group. She recognised a few familiar faces from around the district, but many people there were strangers.

Very soon one of them would be the new owner of Windaroo.

She felt so sick she was trembling. Beside her, Roy cleared his throat, folded and unfolded his arms, crossed and uncrossed his legs, as if he couldn't get comfortable.

'I thought Gabe would be here,' he said.

Not trusting her voice to work, she simply shook her head.

On the verandah, the auctioneer shuffled his papers, took a pen out of his pocket and scribbled something, then put the pen back. He cleared his throat. 'Ladies and gentlemen, this excellent working property, Windaroo, has been owned by the Delaney family for over sixty years. I think everyone here is familiar with its size, carrying capacity, stock numbers and general condition, but if you want me to run through any details again put your hand up now.'

No one moved. Piper was stiff with dread. *I'm sorry, Grandad. I know this isn't what you wanted.*

'I'll proceed, then. Windaroo is estimated to carry a market value of—'

Behind them, there was the sound of a motor and tyres crunching on gravel. The auctioneer paused mid-sentence. Heads swivelled. Piper heard Roy's gasp of surprise and looked over her shoulder to see Gabe climbing out of a car. Her heart slammed hard against the wall of her chest as he swung his door shut and took long, loping strides across the lawn towards them.

'Morning,' he said quietly as he sat in the empty chair next to her.

'Hello.' She tried to smile but it was beyond her.

The auctioneer frowned at Gabe, then continued his preamble. 'As I was saying, this property is valued at between nine hundred thousand and a million dollars.'

Gabe sat very still, but when he sensed her watching him he managed to send her a wink and to squeeze her hand. 'Thought you could do with some moral support,' he said.

'Thanks.'

The auctioneer called, 'Do we have someone who'll

open with a starting bid of seven hundred thousand dollars?'

Karl Findley raised his beefy hand.

'Thank you, sir. Seven hundred it is. Any advance on seven hundred? Seven hundred and fifty thousand?'

From the far side, a balding, middle-aged man waved a pen.

'I have seven hundred and fifty thousand.' The auctioneer looked back to Findley. Findley nodded. ' Eight hundred thousand.'

Someone else raised a hand and very quickly the bids climbed to nine hundred and fifty thousand. Piper's heartbeats seemed to accelerate with each bid. Perhaps it had been a mistake to come. This was awful!

'Any advance on nine hundred and fifty thousand?' the auctioneer called.

She sensed Gabe move slightly beside her.

'Nine hundred and seventy?'

Gabe gave a one-fingered salute to the auctioneer.

Piper gasped. 'What do you think you're doing?'

He didn't answer or look her way.

'We have nine hundred and seventy thousand dollars to a new bidder at the back,' the auctioneer called.

Gabe's concentration was firmly fixed ahead. She saw a fine film of sweat on his brow, and his profile was so stern he couldn't have looked more serious if he'd been about to embark on a dangerous military mission.

Why on earth was he bidding for Windaroo? He hadn't said anything about this.

And the bidding was still climbing.

Findley remained as keen as ever. Within a matter of minutes it seemed to be a battle between Findley and

Gabe. Findley, who had no doubt made the bulk of his money from stealing other people's cattle. And Gabe.

The bids reached a million dollars.

'How high will you go?' she whispered.

'One point one is my limit,' he muttered out of the side of his mouth.

'One million dollars,' the auctioneer repeated. 'Any advance on one million? A million and fifty? Thank you, sir. One point one million? We have one point one million over here.'

Piper felt Roy's hand reach for hers. They sat, hands clasped tightly, waiting for Findley to bid past Gabe's offer.'

'One point one five?' The auctioneer's eyes flicked from Findley to Gabe and back again. 'One point one five it is,' he said, acknowledging Findley's bid, and Piper felt sharp disappointment prickle behind her eyes and in her throat.

Roy's hand squeezed even tighter.

For a harrowing, short space of time, her hopes had been raised.

'One point two?' came the auctioneer's voice.

Gabe sat, still as an iceberg.

'I'm looking for an advance on one point one five. Do we have a bid of one point two million dollars?'

Gabe nodded.

'Oh, my God, Gabe, you can't,' Piper whispered, horrified.

He shot her a silencing frown.

Once again the auctioneer looked at Findley. 'Do you wish to bid against one point two million dollars?'

Findley raised a fat finger.

The auctioneer's voice dropped several decibels, but

everyone was so still he could easily be heard. 'So we have a new bid of one point two five. Any advance? Do I hear one point three million dollars for Windaroo station?'

The deathly hush seemed to go on for ever. Everyone present knew the price was being pushed beyond the market value. Piper closed her eyes, unable to stand the tension. She wished she was a fainting kind of woman. How nice it would be to black out now and wake up when this was all over.

'Going once? Going twice? One point three million at the back.'

Her eyes flew open and she stared at Gabe. *Was he crazy?*

There was an eruption down at the front. Karl Findley's wife leapt to her feet, her face beetroot-red. 'You bid higher than that, Karl, and it's the last you'll see of me.' She bent low and hissed something in his ear before stomping away towards their parked car.

The back of Findley's neck flushed as red as her face as he scowled after her and muttered a curse. An excited mumble skittered through the crowd.

The auctioneer shot a perplexed frown towards Findley. 'Are you raising your bid?'

For a full minute Findley sat without moving. It was the longest sixty seconds of Piper's life.

'Sir?'

At last Karl Findley shook his head.

Once more the auctioneer looked around at his assembled audience. 'For the last time, any advance on one point three million? This is your last chance, ladies and gentlemen. It's going…going…Windaroo is sold for one million, three hundred thousand dollars to the gentleman at the back!'

Piper couldn't breathe. She felt exactly as she had at the age of eleven when she'd been thrown from her horse—dumped on the hard, unforgiving ground—shocked and winded.

Stunned.

All around her people were talking, getting out of their seats and moving away. Roy was patting her on the back, but she barely noticed him or the people who nodded and smiled at her. Her eyes were fixed on Gabe as he rose slowly to his feet and strolled past a hunched and morose Findley towards the verandah to speak to the auctioneer. She watched them talking together, nodding, shaking hands. Saw him glance back in her direction.

Gabe Rivers had bought Windaroo! If one of her heifers had strolled up to her and wished her good morning she couldn't have been more stunned. Her mind was struggling to take it in.

Roy was beaming at her. 'Fancy that! I never thought Gabe might buy this place for you, Piper.'

'For me?' She stared at him blankly. 'I don't know that he's bought it for me.' Her voice was barely above a faint whisper.

'Of course he's bought it for you.' Roy joggled her elbow as Gabe walked slowly back to them. 'Are you going to thank him?'

'I—I can't think what I should do.'

Roy shook his head. 'Well, I'm going to scarper and let you two sort this out. But I should think a little appreciation wouldn't go astray.'

As Roy slipped away long legs in blue jeans stopped

in front of Piper. She looked up. Gabe was smiling down at her. 'It's all settled. Windaroo is ours.'

'Ours?' It came out as a squeak.

'Yep.'

'You mean *ours* as in we're both owners?'

'That's right. Piper Fleur O'Malley and Gabriel Martin Rivers—joint owners of what will be the Windaroo Pastoral Company.'

'But I don't understand. One point three million dollars! And you've just bought a helicopter. Can you afford this as well?'

'Almost—I had my pay-out from the army and I cashed in some shares.'

'Not your shares in Edenvale?'

'It doesn't matter.'

'But you went two hundred thousand dollars over your limit—past Windaroo's market value.'

'Well…the property market in Sydney is booming at the moment. I can sell my apartment there any time I want to.'

She covered her face with her hands. He'd gone to all this trouble and expense! 'Oh, my God, Gabe,' she whispered. 'You could have kept your money and shared this property with me for free if I'd accepted your marriage proposal.'

'I am aware of that.' Looping fingers and thumbs loosely around her wrists, he pulled her hands away from her face, and when she raised her gaze to meet his, something in his slow smile sent a trembling thrill skittering down her spine. 'Don't feel too badly, corn cob. I intend to get my money back.'

'How?'

'Let's go inside, where we can talk about this in private.'

Dazed and bewildered, she scrambled quickly to her feet. She tried to tell herself it was too soon to be relieved. She needed to sort this bewildering situation out. Now. In the open. But he was hurrying up the three broad steps to the verandah, through the wide French doors and into the lounge room.

She followed him inside.

Her heart hammered as she watched Gabe close the doors and draw the curtains. Surely this wasn't necessary? The cars outside were moving away. What kind of private discussion did he have in mind?

Hands hitched loosely on his hips, he stood in the middle of her lounge room and seemed to fill it with his height and his wide, wide shoulders. Was he really that big, or had she been living with stooped, elderly men for so long that she'd lost her sense of proportion? 'Do you want to take a seat? Where would you like to sit to—um—explain?'

'Right here is fine,' he said, taking a step towards her.

'Here?' she whispered as he took another step.

'Here,' he repeated, taking a final step that brought him so close he was spanning her hips with his hands before she fully realised what was happening.

The dark warmth in his eyes turned her insides hollow.

'Gabe, what's going on?'

His hands moved possessively around her and he drew her into him. 'What's going on? I'm going to kiss you,' he murmured.

'What?' Was this another of his strange lessons? With a sob that was half-confusion, half-regret, she pushed her hands flat against his chest. 'You might have bought Windaroo, but I can't be bought, Gabe…' Her voice trailed off as he ignored her protest and brushed his beautiful mouth slowly over hers.

'Shh. Trust me.'

*Trust him?*

She'd been trusting Gabe all her life. Trustworthy was his middle name. Just the same…

'Let me explain this my way,' he said, and before she could argue he was drawing her lower lip between both his…

His way. Oh, man! Gabe was tasting her, teasing her, and his mouth was warm and steady and showed no sign of leaving. His lips moulded and blended and moved with hers, making her feel like a rosy dawn, growing pink and warm and full of light.

He ran his tongue along her parted lips and she began to melt from the toes up. *Oh, Gabe.* A little sigh escaped and she silently pleaded for more.

'Piper, I want you to keep Windaroo.'

'But why? I still don't quite understand.'

His smile was pure Gabe. 'Because of this, sugar plum.'

Gently, gently, he took the tip of her tongue between his teeth, and as he did she heard his soft, helpless groan. She'd never imagined such a vulnerable, needy, sexy sound. Gabe kissed her hungrily, his hands cradling her face, and she couldn't hold back, couldn't stop herself from kissing him and kissing him and *kissing* him. The warm rosiness inside her became a flood of heat, a shared hotness fluxing between them, mounting in delicious intensity, turning their kiss into a wild mating of lips and tongues.

And still she wanted more! She raised her hands to his shoulders so she could pull herself hard against him. Too much denim in the way! A feverish impatience told her she wouldn't be satisfied until they were as close as a man and a woman could possibly be.

He trailed heated lips over her chin and down her throat, till he reached the neckline of her blouse. He nipped at it impatiently. 'I want to kiss all of you, Piper.'

'Yes,' came her breathless answer.

He cupped her chin and tipped it up, so that she was looking clear into his eyes—his dark green, fiercely beautiful eyes. They were so close she could see little flecks of hazel. She could see his black, spiky lashes. Gabe's eyes, the dearest eyes in the whole world, were speaking to her, shining, brimming with deep, deep emotion.

His gaze held hers for the longest time, then his mouth quirked into a shy, boyish smile as he stepped back a little and lifted his hands to the top button on his shirt.

He undid the button. 'There's something I have to show you,' he murmured.

She felt a sudden flurry of panic. Her cheeks burned as he undid the small blue buttons, and her legs almost caved in as the fabric fell apart to reveal the broad, tanned expanse of his chest with its short, springy hair.

He reached the lowest button, just above the waistband of his jeans, and sent her another wary smile as he tugged the shirt-tails free. Then, with a shrug of his shoulders, he discarded the garment.

When he stood before her she sucked in a swift breath. Gabe had always been athletic and fit, and his years in the army had built and honed him so that his shoulders were broader than ever, his biceps more bulging, his torso leaner and more tightly packed.

But the accident had wrought changes, too.

The line of a deep, red, angry scar cut across the biceps of his bronzed right arm, pooling and spreading over his shoulder and then scouring along the line of his collarbone. There was another smaller scar over the ribs on his left side. Instinctively, she reached up to touch gentle fingertips to his shoulder.

Raising her eyes, she caught a fierce, guarded uncertainty in his face. Tears prickled behind her eyelids, and on impulse she pressed her lips to the ridge of scar tissue, kissed her way along it as he had kissed her neck seconds earlier.

'Piper,' came his broken cry, and he cradled her head against his wounded shoulder. She felt his chest heaving against hers and her heart almost broke.

'You didn't think I'd give two hoots about some little old scars, did you?'

'I needed to be sure.'

'I could never mind anything about you, Gabe.'

She was rewarded by another kiss, deeper and even more passionate than the last. And now there was the incredible pleasure of being held against his beautiful, bare, masculine chest as well as the wild, wonderful sensation of having his mouth locked with hers.

When he broke the kiss, he said into her ear, 'Now my jeans, Piper. I need you to see it all.' Without another word he bent down, pulled off his riding boots and socks and kicked them aside, then stood before her, smiling cautiously.

His jeans. Gabe Rivers's jeans. Piper gulped. He wasn't wearing a belt, so it was a simple matter of him unsnapping the metal stud and lowering the zip. Simple. Yeah, right. As if she'd watched a score of sexy men undress right in front of her—and in the privacy of her own home.

Under any other circumstances shyness might have forced her to look elsewhere. But it was time to cast shyness aside. Time to be honest. Completely honest. This was Gabe at his most vulnerable.

She held his gaze as he unsnapped the fastener and lowered the zip.

Could he hear the racing of her heart? Had he any idea of the way her blood was pulsing through her as his jeans slipped away to reveal the dark trail of hair leading down into his cotton boxer shorts? Did he notice her deep blush when she saw the obvious evidence of his arousal?

She saw his legs and swallowed a gasp. His right leg was very bad. A thick, violet-red slash tore its way down his thigh, almost covering his knee and continuing down his calf. His ankle was a mass of scar tissue.

In hospital, whenever she'd visited, this leg had been hidden by plaster. She felt a wave of hot anger. How unfair that he'd risked his body countless times on dangerous military missions and yet a careless civilian could do this to him!

Her eyes filled with tears.

His jaw thrust forward. 'So now you know,' he said gruffly. 'I'm a damaged man.'

He looked away, but not before she saw the hurt in his eyes. Heavens! Did he think she minded? Blinking rapidly to rid herself of tears, she stepped closer. 'No scars can mar you, Gabe. As far as I'm concerned, you're perfect.'

'I'm hardly that, Piper.'

She touched his chin and turned his face till she could look into his eyes. 'Believe me, Gabe Rivers, you're perfect.' She wound her arms around his neck and raised her lips to kiss the underside of his jaw. 'Look at all this,' she said huskily as she ran hungry hands over the hard planes of his chest, over his massive shoulders and down the muscled length of his arms. 'Gabe, you're perfect. I'm getting more obsessed every minute.'

He smiled slowly. 'Yeah?'

'Absolutely.' She smiled back at him. 'So it's time you put me out of my misery and explained exactly what this is all about.'

## CHAPTER FOURTEEN

GABE couldn't believe how nervous he felt. Flying night missions over Somalia for the United Nations was a piece of cake compared to facing Piper now.

Everything important was on the line. Everything—including his heart. *Especially* his heart.

Four weeks ago, when Piper walked out on him, she'd forced him to face the unavoidable truth. There'd been no way he could go on pretending she was just a cute kid, a sweet little tagalong. He'd had to accept that the brotherly love he'd felt ever since she was born was forever a thing of the past.

It had started the moment he heard her plans to get married, but he'd been resisting the impossible notion that he wanted her for himself.

And he'd been so busy trying to ignore the strength and depth of his feelings, trying to fight a building hunger for her, that he'd given very little thought to how she felt.

What a dumb ass he'd been to think she'd accept that cold, impersonal marriage proposal on the day she'd come back from the solicitor!

Her rejection had hurt and sent him tearing off to the coast, and his mother had been right about distance. From there he'd seen his life through a wider lens and he'd been hit by the truth.

Piper O'Malley was vital to his happiness. He could only hope to God that he was important to hers.

Fear of failure had never been an issue for him, but

now it clawed at his throat and constricted his breathing. He'd offered to buy Windaroo once before and she'd knocked him back. He'd offered to marry her and she'd refused. He *had* to get this moment right. He couldn't afford another mistake.

His heart thundered in his ears and his hand shook as he traced the sweet curve of her cheek.

'I'm in love with you,' he said, forcing the words past the knot of pain in his throat.

She gave a tiny, choked cry, and he saw a sheen of tears on her upturned face, but, God help him, he couldn't tell if she was happy or horrified by his declaration.

Somehow, he forced himself to go on. 'I got it all wrong last time. I didn't tell you how I felt.'

'No, you didn't,' she whispered, her lips trembling.

'As you pointed out then, I proposed to you from the other side of the room.'

She looked as pale and tense as he felt. 'Are you asking me to marry you? Again?' Her voice quavered on a rising note of disbelief.

To his relief, she didn't protest as he tightened his arms around her. 'Call me stubborn.' He lowered his mouth till it was breathless inches from hers. 'But the fact is I need you, Piper. In my life, in my bed, in my future.' He couldn't resist the urge to brush a lingering caress over her sweet, soft lips. 'I want to get it right this time, so I'm stripped almost bare, with you wrapped in my arms and I'm swearing that I love you, Piper. I'm in love *and* in lust with you.' He kissed her. 'I love you.' He kissed her again. 'I'll love you for ever.'

'Gabe!' Her arms tightened around his neck and she met his kiss with a glad cry. Her mouth welcomed him and she pressed herself close, and then closer, nudging his fears aside. Only the tears on her cheeks and a lingering insecurity made him break the kiss to ask, 'Do I take it this is not a knockback?'

To his horror, she went still in his arms, and her warm, moist lips drifted away from his.

'Piper?'

She took a step back.

'What is it?' he whispered.

She didn't answer, simply stood there, swiping at her tears, looking embarrassed.

'Piper, is something wrong?'

Her answer was a tenuous, tilting smile—a bewildering mixture of shyness and mystery. Gabe felt ill.

Without speaking, she lifted her hands to the scooped neckline of her white linen blouse and undid the first little pearl button. A delicate flush bloomed in her cheeks. 'You went to a lot of trouble to make sure I knew about your scars, Gabe. So this is only fair. You know nothing about my—my body.'

She had to be joking. He'd been checking out every neat line, every pert curve and sweet hollow in her body for weeks now. She would probably be shocked to know how often and in what kind of detail he'd thought about her sexy little shape.

'Sweetheart, I don't need—'

She held up a hand and her blue eyes sparked with a hint of mischief. 'My turn. I get to do this my way,' she said. 'Remember what you told me once? It's too bad for a husband to discover after the wedding that his wife has been shoving socks down her bra.'

Her buttons were slipping undone, giving him teasing glimpses…of soft, pale skin, white lace lingerie, the delicate swell of her breasts.

'Would you like some assistance?' he offered, his

voice rough with the need to reach for her, to peel away every shred of fabric and to discover those breasts for himself. They would be as pale and soft as the rest of her, and tipped with delicate shell-pink.

'My way,' she reminded him as she let the blouse drop to the floor and stood there, blushing profusely and looking up at him from beneath long lashes.

'Check. No socks in here,' she said, running a finger along the lace trim of her low-cut bra.

She was perfect. She was Piper—a unique combination of athleticism and grace mixed with gut-grabbing, pale fragility.

Oh, God, he loved her.

Over the past decade or so he'd been teased relentlessly about the number of women in his life, and there'd been plenty, but he'd never felt so aroused as he did now. *Never.*

She kicked off her boots and socks, just as he had done, and lowered the zip on her jeans, then, taking a deep breath as if she needed an extra burst of courage, she hooked her thumbs beneath the top of her jeans and slid them down over pale smooth hips, delicate white panties and slim thighs.

At first he was so blown away by the poignancy of the moment that he didn't see every detail. Then his eyes hit on the tiny blue horseshoe riding low on her right hip, just above the line of her underwear.

'You have a tattoo.'

She pulled a sheepish grin. 'Do you mind?'

'Are you joking?' He bent down quickly and traced the design with his fingers. 'I love it.' He fought back an urge to kiss it, lick it, eat it. He might frighten her if he showed her exactly how much he liked it. As he straightened again, he asked, 'When did you get it done?'

'When I was sixteen. Remember when I came whingeing to you because Grandad wouldn't let me have a tat? Well, that was the one time I went against your advice and defied both of you. As soon as I went back to boarding school I got it done on my first weekend leave.'

'Did Michael ever know?'

She shook her head. 'Apart from my doctor, you're the first man to witness this.'

'Wow. What an honour.'

'I'm glad you like it, because it'll still be with me when I'm a little old lady of eighty.'

He swallowed. 'Does that mean—are you saying—yes? You'll marry me?'

Piper gasped in surprise. 'Can't you guess? Don't you know I'm crazy in love with you? Why else would I be standing here baring my all? Of course I'm saying yes.' Without waiting another heartbeat, she hurled herself into his arms. 'Yes, Gabe, yes, yes, *yes*!'

They came together hungrily, their longing for each other like a stormburst, breaking through any lingering reserve.

Gabe…her gallant, god-like, gorgeous Gabe. Hers at last. His skin against her skin. His powerful arms binding her to him. His mouth savage as he claimed her. His hands exploring her, urging her closer, even closer.

Each touch, every movement, was like a match striking at flint, and within seconds she was burning with a need that almost frightened her in its intensity.

'Make love to me, Gabe,' she urged softly. 'Please!'

His breathing was ragged and his eyes blazed as he looked down at her. 'Are you sure?'

'Yes!'

Cupping the sides of her face with his hands, his eyes looked deeply into hers and he smiled shakily before he kissed her forehead, her nose, her lips. 'You've no idea how much I love you.'

'It can't possibly be as much as I love you.'

With an impatient, happy groan, he slipped an arm around her shoulders, another beneath her knees and scooped her effortlessly into his arms. As he carried her down the hall she felt dizzy with longing, blissfully weightless and floating.

He turned left and stepped into the airy little green and white room that was her own special haven. A cool breeze drifted through the window, billowing the fine white curtain so that it floated upwards like a bridal veil. The cool air wafted over their heated skin as Gabe let her slide deliciously down his hard body till her feet reached the pale green carpet next to her bed.

Her bed. *Gulp.* She looked up, suddenly shy. 'You won't expect me to know what to do without a little help, will you?'

His eyes glowed warmly as he smiled. With gentle fingers he traced a line down the curve of her cheek, down her neck and out along her collarbone to her shoulder. 'You're exquisite,' he told her, and his hand slowly massaged her shoulder. 'This has nothing to do with performance and everything to do with how we feel about each other.'

'Yes,' she whispered.

He kissed her forehead, her neck, the hollow at the base of her throat. 'How do you feel, Piper?'

'In love. Burning.'

'Me too,' he murmured, nipping gently at her lower lip, drawing it between his teeth, slipping his arms around her once more, deepening the kiss so that his tongue moved slow and sure, twining, delving, dancing with hers.

And once again warm wanting built inside her. He kissed her shoulder, nuzzled her chin, her earlobe, her eyelids, before returning to her mouth, and as she wound her arms around his neck his hands traced slow circles on the skin at her waist. Beautiful, gentle, widening circles that spread like ripples in a pond and skimmed over her hips, her bottom, the underside of her breasts. She felt liquid and warm, like honey melting and dissolving in heated milk.

'Oh, Gabe, that's so nice. It's just the way you told me.'

'How's that?'

'Remember when you explained about touch and taste?'

'Ah, yes.' His thumbs stroked over her wispy lace bra, grazing her nipples, returning two, three times, each time lingering just a little longer.

'Oh,' she sighed.

'You like that?'

'Mmm. I'll die if you stop.'

He kissed her again and unclipped her bra, and as it fell away she heard his soft moan.

'They're not too small?'

'Never.'

His thumb returned to tease her again, making her warm and aching and trembling. Lambent heat flowed like a running flame from her breasts to low inside her. Her legs felt limp and loose. She wanted Gabe, needed him, trusted him, loved him. Had to have him closer. She pulled him with her back towards her bed, longing at last to have the full length of his long, hard body pressing against hers.

'This is where I want you,' she told him. 'And I'm not afraid.'

'I am,' he said. 'I feel like I've never done this before.'

'Good.' She reached up and traced his jaw with her hand and smiled wickedly. 'Don't worry, Gabe. I'll be very gentle with you.'

On the faded blue bedspread in the big bedroom that had been her grandfather's lay a bouquet of white, cream and delicate pink roses.

Piper stood in front of the big oval mirror and slipped her mother's pearl and diamond earrings into her ears. She looked at her reflection and was happy.

She'd chosen her wedding dress without April's help, and although it was the first dress she'd tried on she'd known immediately it was what she wanted. The bodice was slim-fitting and sleeveless, with a wide-scooped neck, and the skirt—silk organza over stiffened taffeta—was wide and full and unashamedly romantic.

Around her wrist was Gabe's wedding gift—a fine gold chain with a sapphire locket fashioned in the shape of a horseshoe. 'It's apparently good luck for a bride to have a horseshoe, but the truth is I'm addicted to them these days,' he'd told her.

Smiling at the memory, she turned to lift the bouquet from the bed and saw Roy hovering in the doorway, blinking and wiping his eyes. He was wearing a brand-new dark suit and his few remaining strands of hair were slicked down very carefully.

'Roy, what an old hunkster! You look terrific.'

'Thanks, Piper.' He took a big white handkerchief

from his trouser pocket, dabbed at his watery eyes and blew his nose. 'I was just thinking the same about you. You look fan-bloody-tastic.'

'Thanks.' She shot a glance back to the mirror, seeking reassurance. 'I hope Gabe will think so.'

'Of course he will. He'll be tickled pink.' He forced a quavery smile. 'Old Michael would have been so proud.'

His words brought a painful lump to her throat. She quickly closed her eyes while she dragged in a deep, fortifying breath. 'Now, that's enough of the sentimental stuff, mate. We can't have waterworks from a bride on her wedding day. I spent all last night crying for Grandad and my parents, wishing they could be here with me.' She forced a fleeting smile. 'Today I've got to concentrate on my future.'

'You're right, love. I'm sorry.' After a moment's awkward silence, Roy brightened and winked at her. 'Hey, I've got some news that'll cheer you up.'

'What's that?'

'Yesterday the police arrested Karl Findley on an extradition warrant from Western Australia. He's going to do some serious time over there for a string of proven cattle duffing offences up in the Kimberley. I had to leg-rope Gabe to stop him from racing in here and telling you.'

She whirled on him. 'You've seen Gabe?'

'Yep, he's here, love, raring to get hitched.'

'How is he? How does he look?'

Grinning, he raised his hands with his thumbs up. 'He looks great, Piper. He'd leave any one of those pretty boy movie actors for dead.'

'Oh, I can't wait to see him.'

'He'll make your little heart shoot right through the roof.'

They shared a happy, conspiratorial smile. Over the past six weeks Gabe had spent much of his time at Windaroo, and Roy was well aware of just how in love he and Piper were.

'There are some spruce-looking army mates of Gabe's out there, too,' he added. 'Some with American accents, and all sorts of fancy-looking women.'

'I suppose there are.' A little spurt of panic sent jittery waves from her stomach to her chest. Gabe had reassured her that his friends would love her. And his mother, Eleanor, had reassured her that the Mullinjim caterers had everything for the reception under control. She had to stay calm. Calm, happy, unflustered, serene.

*As if.*

'Tell me, Roy, do I have my veil on straight?'

He walked nervously around her, studying her head and the hang of the veil from every angle. 'Far as I can tell,' he said. 'But I'm no expert on wedding veils, Piper. I'm afraid I know absolutely flaming nothing about weddings!' The poor fellow's eyes bulged and his Adam's apple slid up and down in his skinny throat. 'I hope I don't stuff this up for you, love.'

'Oh, Roy, don't worry. You're going to be perfect. You just take me by the arm and walk me down the verandah, down the front steps to the jacaranda tree, and hand me over to Gabe. Reverend Parker will look after the rest.' She picked up a tissue from the box on the bedside table and blotted his face, then dropped a quick kiss on his cheek. 'I'm just so thrilled to have you here to give me away.'

Roy's eyes were watery again. He blinked. 'It's an honour, Piper. A real honour. I'm downright proud.'

She cast a quick glance to the antique travel clock on the dressing table and said, 'It's time.'

With a shaky smile, Roy offered her the crook of his elbow. She slipped her arm through his. 'Let's go,' she said.

Piper didn't look at the assembled guests as they walked out onto Windaroo's verandah. All she could see was Gabe, standing beneath the fairytale bluebell flowers of the jacaranda tree, looking tall and gorgeous in his dark suit. He had his back to her, and she fixed her eyes on his short dark hair and the neat white line of his crisp shirt collar, startling in its whiteness against his sun-tanned neck.

Then, as a string quartet struck up the opening chords of the 'Wedding March,' he turned to see her. His face broke into his familiar, heart-stopping smile. A smile that was nurtured by the past and fuelled by the promise of their happiness ahead. She touched the little sapphire horseshoe at her wrist, and with an answering smile whispered to Roy, 'Take me to my man.'

# EPILOGUE

GABE walked back from the stockyards towards Windaroo homestead. His home. The low-set house surrounded by shady verandahs sprawled like a sleepy dog beneath a wide, bright blue outback sky.

Behind him a flock of noisy galahs squabbled in the trees along the creek. The tang of freshly ploughed earth from a nearby paddock filled his nostrils and his riding boots were covered with red dust. And he was happy.

This renewed sense of belonging in the outback could still catch him by surprise, but of course living on Windaroo meant living with Piper, and that made all the difference.

He entered the house, showered, and made a beeline for the kitchen. *En route*, he noticed that Piper had already set the dining table, making it extra elegant for his mother's birthday celebration this evening. The hand-painted dinnerware they'd received as a wedding present was teamed with a matching linen tablecloth and their best silver cutlery. A vase of Eleanor's favourite red roses brightened the table's centre.

As he stepped into the kitchen Piper turned from the sink, where she was hulling strawberries, and her blue eyes danced as she smiled at him. Lord, he loved this woman. Not a day went past when he didn't thank his lucky stars that she'd married him.

'Everything looks and smells great,' he said as he reached over, selected a juicy strawberry and popped it into his mouth. 'What's for dinner?'

'Racks of lamb with green peas, minted wine jelly and hashed brown potatoes, and strawberry shortcake for dessert. I've surpassed myself,' she said proudly. 'They're all your mother's favourites.'

'Glad my mother has such great taste.' His hands rested lightly on her shoulders. 'Good taste runs in the family.' Gently he nuzzled her neck, just below her ear, but as he reached for another strawberry Piper gave his hand a playful smack.

'Hands off. Roy and Bella have been raiding the strawberry patch again, and I need every one of these to decorate the cake.'

'I've no intention of keeping my hands off,' he murmured, and to prove his point he wrapped his arms around her and lightly rubbed her bulging tummy. 'How's my favourite pregnant lady?'

'Bursting with energy at the moment,' she said, dimpling as he kissed the hollow at the base of her neck. She turned in his arms so she could look up at him. 'That's why I insisted on having this birthday dinner for Eleanor today, before it's too late. I felt an incredible burst of energy like this the week before Bella was born, so you'd better not fly too far away over the next week. I might need you.'

'I won't budge from Windaroo,' he promised. 'Anyway, I won't need to. I finally have my team so well organised they can run the whole chopper fleet without me.'

'Good.' Piper kissed the underside of his jaw. 'Because I don't plan on having this baby without you.'

Gabe traced the soft line of her cheek and kissed the tip of her nose. 'Try to keep me away, shortcake.'

There was the sound of a car in the yard outside, and suddenly their kiss was interrupted by a whirlwind charging through the kitchen—a whirlwind made up of a small human being and several half-grown puppies.

'What the devil—?' cried Gabe.

'Grandma! Grandpa!' shouted his four-year-old daughter.

'Hey!' he shouted back. 'Bella! Stop! Right now!'

A tiny figure in jeans and a hot pink T-shirt pivoted in the kitchen doorway, and from beneath a fringe of corn-gold hair green eyes glared at him. Three blue heeler puppies yapped and leapt in happy confusion, their tails wagging madly.

His daughter called to him over their noise. 'I can't stop, Daddy. Grandma's here.'

'You will stop!' Gabe replied firmly.

'But Grandpa and Uncle Jonno are here, too. They'll be *dying* to see me.'

Gabe crossed the kitchen, opened the screen door and shooed the pups outside, then closed the door again. 'They'll live a little longer while I talk to you, Bella. I thought I told you you're not to have those dogs inside the house. You've had them in your bedroom again, haven't you?'

Her full bottom lip protruded stubbornly. 'Tom, Dick and Harry was lonely.'

'But I've told you before, they're working dogs. They have to learn to muster cattle. We don't want to spoil them.'

Two plump pink hands sat on her little hips. 'But, Daddy, it's Sunday. Workers get the day off on Sunday, don't they?'

Gabe's mouth twitched, but he managed to hold back an urge to smile as he knelt in front of his daughter. Big mistake. At this level her moss-green eyes looked directly at him. Apart from her eyes, which were like his, she was a diminutive version of Piper. With Piper's determination and spirit. And, as always, his heart melted. 'I guess they can come in to play on Sundays, sprout. But only for a few more weeks until they start training.'

He was rewarded by a huge grin and a bear hug. Then Bella was gone, flying across the verandah to greet his family.

'You're nothing but an old softie,' Piper said with a smile.

As he straightened again, Gabe shrugged. 'She's a chip off the old block, Piper, and I've always been soft on you.'

'Thank heavens,' she said, opening her arms to him. And, before his family arrived, they finished the kiss their daughter had interrupted.

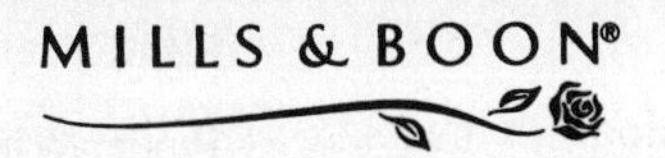


# FEBRUARY 2003 HARDBACK TITLES

## ROMANCE™

| Title | Code | ISBN |
|---|---|---|
| **The Pregnancy Proposal** *Helen Bianchin* | H5748 | 0 263 17595 2 |
| **Alejandro's Revenge** *Anne Mather* | H5749 | 0 263 17596 0 |
| **Marco's Pride** *Jane Porter* | H5750 | 0 263 17645 2 |
| **City Cinderella** *Catherine George* | H5751 | 0 263 17646 0 |
| **A Sicilian Husband** *Kate Walker* | H5752 | 0 263 17647 9 |
| **Blackmailed by the Boss** *Kathryn Ross* | H5753 | 0 263 17648 7 |
| **At the Millionaire's Bidding** *Lee Wilkinson* | H5754 | 0 263 17649 5 |
| **A Spanish Inheritance** *Susan Stephens* | H5755 | 0 263 17650 9 |
| **Rush to the Altar** *Rebecca Winters* | H5756 | 0 263 17651 7 |
| **The Venetian Playboy's Bride** *Lucy Gordon* | H5757 | 0 263 17652 5 |
| **Her Secret Millionaire** *Jodi Dawson* | H5758 | 0 263 17653 3 |
| **A Wedding at Windaroo** *Barbara Hannay* | H5759 | 0 263 17654 1 |
| **Traveling Man** *Leigh Michaels* | H5760 | 0 263 17655 X |
| **The Heiress Bride** *Laurey Bright* | H5761 | 0 263 17656 8 |
| **Delivering Secrets** *Fiona McArthur* | H5762 | 0 263 17657 6 |
| **His Emergency Fiancée** *Kate Hardy* | H5763 | 0 263 17658 4 |

## HISTORICAL ROMANCE™

| Title | Code | ISBN |
|---|---|---|
| **An Unconventional Heiress** *Paula Marshall* | H545 | 0 263 17821 8 |
| **Kitty** *Elizabeth Bailey* | H546 | 0 263 17822 6 |

## MEDICAL ROMANCE™

| Title | Code | ISBN |
|---|---|---|
| **Daisy and the Doctor** *Meredith Webber* | M463 | 0 263 17845 5 |
| **The Surgeon's Marriage** *Maggie Kingsley* | M464 | 0 263 17846 3 |

# FEBRUARY 2003 LARGE PRINT TITLES

## ROMANCE™

| Title | No. | ISBN |
|---|---|---|
| **The Contaxis Baby** *Lynne Graham* | 1551 | 0 263 17875 7 |
| **Marco's Convenient Wife** *Penny Jordan* | 1552 | 0 263 17876 5 |
| **Sarah's Secret** *Catherine George* | 1553 | 0 263 17877 3 |
| **The Italian's Demand** *Sara Wood* | 1554 | 0 263 17878 1 |
| **A Professional Marriage** *Jessica Steele* | 1555 | 0 263 17879 X |
| **The Baby Bombshell** *Day Leclaire* | 1556 | 0 263 17880 3 |
| **Accidental Bride** *Darcy Maguire* | 1557 | 0 263 17881 1 |
| **The Sheikh's Proposal** *Barbara McMahon* | 1558 | 0 263 17882 X |

## HISTORICAL ROMANCE™

| Title | No. | ISBN |
|---|---|---|
| **Jack Compton's Luck** *Paula Marshall* | 243 | 0 263 17989 3 |
| **The Duke's Mistress** *Ann Elizabeth Cree* | 244 | 0 263 17990 7 |

## MEDICAL ROMANCE™

| Title | No. | ISBN |
|---|---|---|
| **Accidental Seduction** *Caroline Anderson* | 449 | 0 263 17967 2 |
| **The Spanish Doctor** *Margaret Barker* | 450 | 0 263 17968 0 |
| **The ER Affair** *Leah Martyn* | 451 | 0 263 17969 9 |
| **Emergency: Doctor in Need** *Lucy Clark* | 452 | 0 263 17970 2 |

0103 Gen Std LP

# MARCH 2003 HARDBACK TITLES

## ROMANCE™

| Title | Code | ISBN |
|---|---|---|
| **The Billionaire Bridegroom** *Emma Darcy* | H5764 | 0 263 17659 2 |
| **The Sheikh's Virgin Bride** *Penny Jordan* | H5765 | 0 263 17660 6 |
| **An Enigmatic Man** *Carole Mortimer* | H5766 | 0 263 17661 4 |
| **At the Playboy's Pleasure** *Kim Lawrence* | H5767 | 0 263 17662 2 |
| **Nathan's Child** *Anne McAllister* | H5768 | 0 263 17663 0 |
| **Mother and Mistress** *Kay Thorpe* | H5769 | 0 263 17664 9 |
| **Midnight Rhythms** *Karen van der Zee* | H5770 | 0 263 17665 7 |
| **The Boss's Urgent Proposal** *Susan Meier* | H5771 | 0 263 17666 5 |
| **The Independent Bride** *Sophie Weston* | H5772 | 0 263 17667 3 |
| **The Ordinary Princess** *Liz Fielding* | H5773 | 0 263 17668 1 |
| **Fiancé Wanted Fast!** *Jessica Hart* | H5774 | 0 263 17669 X |
| **Baby Chase** *Hannah Bernard* | H5775 | 0 263 17670 3 |
| **True Love, Inc.** *Jackie Braun* | H5776 | 0 263 17671 1 |
| **What Child Is This?** *Cara Colter* | H5777 | 0 263 17672 X |
| **The Surgeon's Gift** *Carol Marinelli* | H5778 | 0 263 17673 8 |
| **The Nurse's Child** *Abigail Gordon* | H5779 | 0 263 17674 6 |

## HISTORICAL ROMANCE™

| Title | Code | ISBN |
|---|---|---|
| **The Viking's Captive** *Julia Byrne* | H547 | 0 263 17823 4 |
| **The Unruly Chaperon** *Elizabeth Rolls* | H548 | 0 263 17824 2 |

## MEDICAL ROMANCE™

| Title | Code | ISBN |
|---|---|---|
| **To the Doctor: A Daughter** *Marion Lennox* | M465 | 0 263 17847 1 |
| **A Mother's Special Care** *Jessica Matthews* | M466 | 0 263 17848 X |

MILLS & BOON®

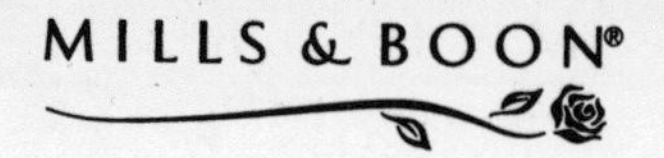

# MARCH 2003 LARGE PRINT TITLES

## ROMANCE™

| Title | No. | ISBN |
|---|---|---|
| **Hot Pursuit** *Anne Mather* | 1559 | 0 263 17883 8 |
| **Wife: Bought and Paid For** *Jacqueline Baird* | 1560 | 0 263 17884 6 |
| **The Forced Marriage** *Sara Craven* | 1561 | 0 263 17885 4 |
| **Mackenzie's Promise** *Catherine Spencer* | 1562 | 0 263 17886 2 |
| **Maybe Married** *Leigh Michaels* | 1563 | 0 263 17887 0 |
| **The Tycoon's Proposition** *Rebecca Winters* | 1564 | 0 263 17888 9 |
| **The Wedding Challenge** *Jessica Hart* | 1565 | 0 263 17889 7 |
| **Assignment: Single Man** *Caroline Anderson* | 1566 | 0 263 17890 0 |

## HISTORICAL ROMANCE™

| Title | No. | ISBN |
|---|---|---|
| **The Earl's Prize** *Nicola Cornick* | 245 | 0 263 17991 5 |
| **Nell** *Elizabeth Bailey* | 246 | 0 263 17992 3 |

## MEDICAL ROMANCE™

| Title | No. | ISBN |
|---|---|---|
| **A Doctor's Honour** *Jessica Matthews* | 453 | 0 263 17971 0 |
| **A Family of Their Own** *Jennifer Taylor* | 454 | 0 263 17972 9 |
| **Paramedic Partners** *Abigail Gordon* | 455 | 0 263 17973 7 |
| **A Doctor's Courage** *Gill Sanderson* | 456 | 0 263 17974 5 |